A Voyage to the Moon

George Tucker

Contents

A VOYAGE TO THE MOON

BY

George Tucker

"It is the very error of the moon,
She comes more near the earth than she was wont,
And makes men mad."--Othello.

APPEAL TO THE PUBLIC.

Having, by a train of fortunate circumstances, accomplished a voyage, of which the history of mankind affords no example; having, moreover, exerted every faculty of body and mind, to make my adventures useful to my countrymen, and even to mankind, by imparting to them the acquisition of secrets in physics and morals, of which they had not formed the faintest conception,--I flattered myself that both in the character of traveller and public benefactor, I had earned for myself an immortal name. But how these fond, these justifiable hopes have been answered, the following narrative will show.

On my return to this my native State, as soon as it was noised abroad that I had met with extraordinary adventures, and made a most wonderful voyage, crowds of people pressed eagerly to see me. I at first met their inquiries with a cautious silence, which, however, but sharpened their curiosity. At length I was visited by a near relation, with whom I felt less disposed to reserve. With friendly solicitude he inquired "how much I had made by my voyage;" and when he was informed that, although I had added to my knowledge, I had not improved my fortune, he stared at me a while, and remarking that he had business at the Bank, as well as an appointment on 'Change, suddenly took his leave. After this, I was not much interrupted by the tribe of inquisitive idlers, but was visited principally by a few men of science, who wished to learn what I could add to their knowledge of nature. To this class I was more communicative; and when I severally informed them that I had actually been to the Moon, some of them shrugged their shoulders, others laughed in my face, and some were angry at my supposed attempt to deceive them; but all, with a single exception, were incredulous.

It was to no purpose that I appealed to my former character for veracity. I was answered, that travelling had changed my morals, as it had changed other people's.

I asked what motives I could have for attempting to deceive them. They replied, the love of distinction--the vanity of being thought to have seen what had been seen by no other mortal; and they triumphantly asked me in turn, what motives Raleigh, and Riley, and Hunter, and a hundred other travellers, had for their misrepresentations. Finding argument thus unavailing, I produced visible and tangible proofs of the truth of my narrative. I showed them a specimen of moonstone. They asserted that it was of the same character as those meteoric stones which had been found in every part of the world, and that I had merely procured a piece of one of these for the purpose of deception. I then exhibited some of what I considered my most curious Lunar plants: but this made the matter worse; for it so happened, that similar ones were then cultivated in Mr. Prince's garden at Flushing. I next produced some rare insects, and feathers of singular birds: but persons were found who had either seen, or read, or heard of similar insects and birds in Hoo-Choo, or Paraguay, or Prince of Wales's Island. In short, having made up their minds that what I said was not true, they had an answer ready for all that I could urge in support of my character; and those who judged most christianly, defended my veracity at the expense of my understanding, and ascribed my conduct to partial insanity.

There was, indeed, a short suspension to this cruel distrust. An old friend coming to see me one day, and admiring a beautiful crystal which I had brought from the Moon, insisted on showing it to a jeweller, who said that it was an unusually hard stone, and that if it were a diamond, it would be worth upwards of 150,000 dollars. I know not whether the mistake that ensued proceeded from my friend, who is something of a wag, or from one of the lads in the jeweller's shop, who, hearing a part of what his master had said, misapprehended the rest; but so it was, that the next day I had more visiters than ever, and among them my kinsman, who was kind enough to stay with me, as if he enjoyed my good fortune, until both the Exchange and the Banks were closed. On the same day, the following paragraph appeared in one of the morning prints:

> "We understand that our enterprising and intelligent traveller,
> JOSEPH ATTERLEY, Esquire, has brought from his Lunar Expedition,
> a diamond of extraordinary size and lustre. Several of the most
> experienced jewellers of this city have estimated it at from

250,000 to 300,000 dollars; and some have gone so far as to say it would be cheap at half a million. We have the authority of a near relative of that gentleman for asserting, that the satisfactory testimonials which he possesses of the correctness of his narrative, are sufficient to satisfy the most incredulous, and to silence malignity itself."

But this gleam of sunshine soon passed away. Two days afterwards, another paragraph appeared in the same paper, in these words:

"We are credibly informed, that the supposed diamond of the *famous* traveller to the Moon, turns out to be one of those which are found on Diamond Island, in Lake George. We have heard that Mr. A----y means to favour the public with an account of his travels, under the title of 'Lunarian Adventures;' but we would take the liberty of recommending, that for **Lunarian**, he substitute **Lunatic**."

Thus disappointed in my expectations, and assailed in my character, what could I do but appeal to an impartial public, by giving them a circumstantial detail of what was most memorable in my adventures, that they might judge, from intrinsic evidence, whether I was deficient either in soundness of understanding or of moral principle? But let me first bespeak their candour, and a salutary diffidence of themselves, by one or two well-authenticated anecdotes.

During the reign of Louis the XIVth, the king of Siam having received an ambassador from that monarch, was accustomed to hear, with wonder and delight, the foreigner's descriptions of his own country: but the minister having one day mentioned, that in France, water, at one time of the year, became a solid substance, the Siamese prince indignantly exclaimed,--"Hold, sir! I have listened to the strange things you have told me, and have hitherto believed them all; but now when you wish to persuade me that water, which I know as well as you, can become hard, I see that your purpose is to deceive me, and I do not believe a word you have uttered."

But as the present patriotic preference for home-bred manufactures, may extend to anecdotes as well as to other productions, a story of domestic origin may have more weight with most of my readers, than one introduced from abroad.

The chief of a party of Indians, who had visited Washington during Mr. Jefferson's presidency, having, on his return home, assembled his tribe, gave them a detail of his adventures; and dwelling particularly upon the courteous treatment the party had received from their "Great Father," stated, among other things, that he had given them ice, though it was then mid-summer. His countrymen, not having the vivacity of our ladies, listened in silence till he had ended, when an aged chief stepped forth, and remarked that he too, when a young man, had visited their Great Father Washington, in New-York, who had received him as a son, and treated him with all the delicacies that his country afforded, but had given him no ice. "Now," added the orator, "if any man in the world could have made ice in the summer, it was Washington; and if he could have made it, I am sure he would have given it to me. Tustanaggee is, therefore, a liar, and not to be believed."

In both these cases, though the argument seemed fair, the conclusion was false; for had either the king or the chief taken the trouble to satisfy himself of the fact, he might have found that his limited experience had deceived him.

It is unquestionably true, that if travellers sometimes impose on the credulity of mankind, they are often also not believed when they speak the truth. Credulity and scepticism are indeed but different names for the same hasty judgment on insufficient evidence: and, as the old woman readily assented that there might be "mountains of sugar and rivers of rum," because she had seen them both, but that there were "fish which could fly," she never would believe; so thousands give credit to Redheiffer's patented discovery of perpetual motion, because they had beheld his machine, and question the existence of the sea-serpent, because they have not seen it.

I would respectfully remind that class of my readers, who, like the king, the Indian, or the old woman, refuse to credit any thing which contradicts the narrow limits of their own observation, that there are "more secrets in nature than are dreamt of in their philosophy;" and that upon their own principles, before they have a right to condemn me, they should go or send to the mountains of Ava, for some of the metal with which I made my venturous experiment, and make one for themselves.

As to those who do not call in question my veracity, but only doubt my sanity, I fearlessly appeal from their unkind judgment to the sober and unprejudiced part of mankind, whether, what I have stated in the following pages, is not consonant with truth and nature, and whether they do not there see, faithfully reflected from the Moon, the errors of the learned on Earth, and "the follies of the wise?"

JOSEPH ATTERLEY.
Long-Island, September, 1827.

CHAPTER I.

Atterley's birth and education--He makes a voyage--Founders off the Burman coast--Adventures in that Empire--Meets with a learned Brahmin
from Benares.

Being about to give a narrative of my singular adventures to the world,
which, I foresee, will be greatly divided about their authenticity, I will
premise something of my early history, that those to whom I am not personally known, may be better able to ascertain what credit is due to the
facts which rest only on my own assertion.

I was born in the village of Huntingdon, on Long-Island, on the 11th day of
May, 1786. Joseph Atterley, my father, formerly of East Jersey, as it was once called,
had settled in this place about a year before, in consequence of having married
my mother, Alice Schermerhorn, the only daughter of a snug Dutch farmer in the
neighbourhood. By means of the portion he received with my mother, together with
his own earnings, he was enabled to quit the life of a sailor, to which he had been
bred, and to enter into trade. After the death of his father-in-law, by whose will he
received a handsome accession to his property, he sought, in the city of New-York,
a theatre better suited to his enlarged capital. He here engaged in foreign trade; and,
partaking of the prosperity which then attended American commerce, he gradually
extended his business, and finally embarked in our new branch of traffic to the East
Indies and China. He was now very generally respected, both for his wealth and fair
dealing; was several years a director in one of the insurance offices; was president
of the society for relieving the widows and orphans of distressed seamen; and, it is
said, might have been chosen alderman, if he had not refused, on the ground that
he did not think himself qualified.

My father was not one of those who set little value on book learning, from their own consciousness of not possessing it: on the contrary, he would often remark, that as he felt the want of a liberal education himself, he was determined to bestow one on me. I was accordingly, at an early age, put to a grammar school of good repute in my native village, the master of which, I believe, is now a member of Congress; and, at the age of seventeen, was sent to Princeton, to prepare myself for some profession. During my third year at that place, in one of my excursions to Philadelphia, and for which I was always inventing pretexts, I became acquainted with one of those faces and forms which, in a youth of twenty, to see, admire, and love, is one and the same thing. My attentions were favourably received. I soon became desperately in love; and, in spite of the advice of my father and entreaties of my mother, who had formed other schemes for me nearer home, I was married on the anniversary of my twenty-first year.

It was not until the first trance of bliss was over, that I began to think seriously on the course of life I was to pursue. From the time that my mind had run on love and matrimony, I had lost all relish for serious study; and long before that time, I had felt a sentiment bordering on contempt for the pursuits of my father. Besides, he had already taken my two younger brothers into the counting-house with him. I therefore prevailed on my indulgent parent, with the aid of my mother's intercession, to purchase for me a neat country-seat near Huntingdon, which presented a beautiful view of the Sound, and where, surrounded by the scenes of my childhood, I promised myself to realise, with my Susanna, that life of tranquil felicity which fancy, warmed by love, so vividly depicts.

If we did not meet with all that we had expected, it was because we had expected too much. The happiest life, like the purest atmosphere, has its clouds as well as its sunshine; and what is worse, we never fully know the value of the one, until we have felt the inconvenience of the other. In the cultivation of my farm--in educating our children, a son and two daughters, in reading, music, painting--and in occasional visits to our friends in New-York and Philadelphia, seventeen years glided swiftly and imperceptibly away; at the end of which time death, in depriving me of an excellent wife, made a wreck of my hopes and enjoyments. For the purpose of seeking that relief to my feelings which change of place only could afford, I determined to make a sea voyage; and, as one of my father's vessels was about to sail for Canton, I accordingly embarked on board the well-known ship the *Two Brothers*, captain Thomas, and left Sandy-hook on the 5th day of June, 1822, having first placed my three children under the care of my brother William.

I will not detain the reader with a detail of the first incidents of our voyage, though they were sufficiently interesting at the time they occurred, and were not wanting in the usual variety. We had, in singular succession, dead calms and fresh breezes, stiff gales and sudden squalls; saw sharks, flying-fish, and dolphins; spoke several vessels: had a visit from Neptune when we crossed the Line, and were compelled to propitiate his favour with some gallons of spirits, which he seems always to find a very agreeable change from sea water; and touched at Table Bay and at Madagascar.

On the whole, our voyage was comparatively pleasant and prosperous, until the 24th of October; when, off the mouths of the Ganges, after a fine clear autumnal day, just about sunset, a small dark speck was seen in the eastern horizon by our experienced and watchful captain, who, after noticing it for a few moments, pronounced that we should have a hurricane. The rapidity with which this speck grew into a dense cloud, and spread itself in darkness over the heavens, as well as the increasing swell of the ocean before we felt the wind, soon convinced us he was right. No time was lost in lowering our topmasts, taking double reefs, and making every thing snug, to meet the fury of the tempest. I thought I had already witnessed all that was terrific on the ocean; but what I had formerly seen, had been mere child's play compared with this. Never can I forget the impression that was made upon me by the wild uproar of the elements. The smooth, long swell of the waves gradually changed into an agitated frothy surface, which constant flashes of lightning presented to us in all its horror; and in the mean time the wind whistled through the rigging, and the ship creaked as if she was every minute going to pieces.

About midnight the storm was at its height, and I gave up all for lost. The wind, which first blew from the south-west, was then due south, and the sailors said it began to abate a little before day: but I saw no great difference until about three in the afternoon; soon after which the clouds broke away, and showed us the sun setting in cloudless majesty, while the billows still continued their stupendous rolling, but with a heavy movement, as if, after such mighty efforts, they were seeking repose in the bosom of their parent ocean. It soon became almost calm; a light western breeze barely swelled our sails, and gently wafted us to the land, which we could faintly discern to the north-east. Our ship had been so shaken in the tempest, and was so leaky, that captain Thomas thought it prudent to make for the first port we could reach.

At dawn we found ourselves in full view of a coast, which, though not personally known to the captain, he pronounced by his charts to be a part of the Burmese Empire, and in the neighbourhood of Mergui, on the Martaban coast. The leak had now increased to an alarming extent, so that we found it would be impossible to carry the ship safe into port. We therefore hastily threw our clothes, papers, and eight casks of silver, into the long-boat; and before we were fifty yards from the ship, we saw her go down. Some of the underwriters in New York, as I have since learnt, had the conscience to contend that we left the ship sooner than was necessary, and have suffered themselves to be sued for the sums they had severally insured. It was a little after midday when we reached the town, which is perched on a high bluff, overlooking the coasts, and contains about a thousand houses, built of bamboo, and covered with palm leaves. Our dress, appearance, language, and the manner of our arrival, excited great surprise among the natives, and the liveliest curiosity; but with these sentiments some evidently mingled no very friendly feelings. The Burmese were then on the eve of a rupture with the East India Company, a fact which we had not before known; and mistaking us for English, they supposed, or affected to suppose, that we belonged to a fleet which was about to invade them, and that our ship had been sunk before their eyes, by the tutelar divinity of the country. We were immediately carried before their governor, or chief magistrate, who ordered our baggage to be searched, and finding that it consisted principally of silver, he had no doubt of our hostile intentions. He therefore sent all of us, twenty-two in number, to prison, separating, however, each one from the rest. My companions were released the following spring, as I have since learnt, by the invading army of Great Britain; but it was my ill fortune (if, indeed, after what has since happened, I can so regard it) to be taken for an officer of high rank, and to be sent, the third day afterwards, far into the interior, that I might be more safely kept, and either used as a hostage or offered for ransom, as circumstances should render advantageous.

The reader is, no doubt, aware that the Burman Empire lies beyond the Ganges, between the British possessions and the kingdom of Siam; and that the natives nearly assimilate with those of Hindostan, in language, manners, religion, and character, except that they are more hardy and warlike.

I was transported very rapidly in a palanquin, (a sort of decorated litter,) carried on the shoulders of four men, who, for greater despatch, were changed every three hours. In this way I travelled thirteen days, in which time we reached a little village in the mountainous district between the Irawaddi and Saloon rivers, where I was placed under the care of an inferior magistrate, called a Mirvoon, who there exercised the chief authority.

This place, named Mozaun, was romantically situated in a fertile valley, that seemed to be completely shut in by the mountains. A small river, a branch of the Saloon, entered it from the west, and, after running about four miles in nearly a straight direction, turned suddenly round a steep hill to the south, and was entirely lost to view. The village was near a gap in the mountain, through which the river seemed to have forced its way, and consisted of about forty or fifty huts, built of the bamboo cane and reeds. The house of my landlord was somewhat larger and better than the rest. It stood on a little knoll that overlooked the village, the valley, the stream that ran through it, and commanded a distant view of the country beyond the gap. It was certainly a lovely little spot, as it now appears to my imagination; but when the landscape was new to me, I was in no humour to relish its beauties, and when my mind was more in a state to appreciate them, they had lost their novelty.

My keeper, whose name was Sing Fou, and who, from a long exercise of magisterial authority, was rough and dictatorial, behaved to me somewhat harshly at first; but my patient submission so won his confidence and good will, that I soon became a great favourite; was regarded more as one of his family than as a prisoner, and was allowed by him every indulgence consistent with my safe custody. But the difficulties in the way of my escape were so great, that little restraint was imposed on my motions. The narrow defile in the gap, through which the river rushed like a torrent, was closed with a gate. The mountains, by which the valley was hemmed in, were utterly impassable, thickly set as they were with jungle, consisting of tangled brier, thorn and forest trees, of which those who have never been in a tropical climate can form no adequate idea. In some places it would be difficult to penetrate more than a mile in the day; during which time the traveller would be perpetually tormented by noxious insects, and in constant dread of beasts of prey.

The only outlet from this village was by passing down the valley along the settlements, and following the course of the stream; so that there was no other injunction laid on me, than not to extend my rambles far in that direction. Sing Fou's household consisted of his wife, whom I rarely saw, four small children, and six servants; and here I enjoyed nearly as great a portion of happiness as in any part of my life.

It had been one of my favourite amusements to ramble towards a part of the western ridge, which rose in a cone about a mile and a half from the village, and there ascending to some comparatively level spot, or point projecting from its side, enjoy the beautiful scenery which lay before me, and the evening breeze, which has such a delicious freshness in a tropical climate.

Nor was this all. In a deep sequestered nook, formed by two spurs of this mountain, there lived a venerable Hindoo, whom the people of the village called the Holy Hermit. The favourable accounts I received of his character, as well as his odd course of life, made me very desirous of becoming acquainted with him; and, as he was often visited by the villagers, I found no difficulty in getting a conductor to his cell. His character for sanctity, together with a venerable beard, might have discouraged advances towards an acquaintance, if his lively piercing eye, a countenance expressive of great mildness and kindness of disposition, and his courteous manners, had not yet more strongly invited it. He was indeed not averse to society, though he had seemed thus to fly from it; and was so great a favourite with his neighbours, that his cell would have been thronged with visitors, but for the difficulty of the approach to it. As it was, it was seldom resorted to, except for the purpose of obtaining his opinion and counsel on all the serious concerns of his neighbours. He prescribed for the sick, and often provided the medicine they required--expounded the law--adjusted disputes--made all their little arithmetical calculations--gave them moral instruction--and, when he could not afford them relief in their difficulties, he taught them patience, and gave them consolation. He, in short, united, for the simple people by whom he was surrounded, the functions of lawyer, physician, schoolmaster, and divine, and richly merited the reverential respect in which they held him, as well as their little presents of eggs, fruit, and garden stuff.

From the first evening that I joined the party which I saw clambering up the

path that led to the Hermit's cell, I found myself strongly attached to this venerable man, and the more so, from the mystery which hung around his history. It was
agreed that he was not a Burmese. None deemed to know certainly where he was
born, or why he came thither. His own account was, that he had devoted himself
to the service of God, and in his pilgrimage over the east, had selected this as a spot
particularly favourable to the life of quiet and seclusion he wished to lead.

There was one part of his story to which I could scarcely give credit. It was
said that in the twelve or fifteen years he had resided in this place, he had been occasionally invisible for months together, and no one could tell why he disappeared,
or whither he had gone. At these times his cell was closed; and although none
ventured to force their way into it, those who were the most prying could hear no
sound indicating that he was within. Various were the conjectures formed on the
subject. Some supposed that he withdrew from the sight of men for the purpose of
more fervent prayer and more holy meditation; others, that he visited his home, or
some other distant country. The more superstitious believed that he had, by a kind
of metempsychosis, taken a new shape, which, by some magical or supernatural
power, he could assume and put off at pleasure. This opinion was perhaps the most
prevalent, as it gained a colour with these simple people, from the chemical and astronomical instruments he possessed. In these he evidently took great pleasure, and
by their means he acquired some of the knowledge by which he so often excited
their admiration.

He soon distinguished me from the rest of his visitors, by addressing questions
to me relative to my history and adventures; and I, in turn, was gratified to have met
with one who took an interest in my concerns, and who alone, of all I had here met
with, could either enter into my feelings or comprehend my opinions. Our conver-
sations were carried on in English, which he spoke with facility and correctness.
We soon found ourselves so much to each other's taste, that there was seldom an
evening that I did not make him a visit, and pass an hour or two in his company.

I learnt from him that he was born and bred at Benares, in Hindostan; that he
had been intended for the priesthood, and had been well instructed in the literature of the east. That a course of untoward circumstances, upon which he seemed
unwilling to dwell, had changed his destination, and made him a wanderer on the
face of the earth. That in the neighbouring kingdom of Siam he had formed an

intimacy with a learned French Jesuit, who had not only taught him his language, but imparted to him a knowledge of much of the science of Europe, its institutions and manners. That after the death of this friend, he had renewed his wanderings; and having been detained in this village by a fit of sickness for some weeks, he was warned that it was time to quit his rambling life. This place being recommended to him, both by its quiet seclusion, and the unsophisticated manners of its inhabitants, he determined to pass the remnant of his days here, and, by devoting them to the purposes of piety, charity, and science, to discharge his duty to his Creator, his species, and himself; "for the love of knowledge," he added, "has long been my chief source of selfish enjoyment."

Our tastes and sentiments accorded in so many points, that our acquaintance ripened by degrees into the closest friendship. We were both strangers--both unfortunate; and were the only individuals here who had any knowledge of letters, or of distant parts of the world. These are, indeed, the main springs of that sympathy, without which there is no love among men. It is being overwise, to treat with contempt what mankind hold in respect: and philosophy teaches us not to extinguish our feelings, but to correct and refine them. My visits to the hermitage were frequently renewed at first, because they afforded me the relief of variety, whilst his intimate knowledge of men and things--his remarkable sagacity and good sense--his air of mingled piety and benignity,--cheated me into forgetfulness of my situation. As these gradually yielded to the lenitive power of time, I sought his conversation for the positive pleasure it afforded, and at last it became the chief source of my happiness. Day after day, and month after month, glided on in this gentle, unvarying current, for more than three years; during which period he had occasionally thrown out dark hints that the time would come when I should be restored to liberty, and that he had an important secret, which he would one day communicate. I should have been more tantalized with the expectations that these remarks were calculated to raise, had I not suspected them to be a good-natured artifice, to save me from despondency, as they were never made except when he saw me looking serious and thoughtful.

CHAPTER II.

The Brahmin's illness--He reveals an important secret to Atterley-- Curious information concerning the Moon--The Glonglims--They plan a voyage to the Moon.

About this period, one afternoon in the month of March, when I repaired to the hermitage as usual, I found my venerable friend stretched on his humble pallet, breathing very quickly, and seemingly in great pain. He was labouring under a pleurisy, which is not unfrequent in the mountainous region, at this season. He told me that his disease had not yielded to the ordinary remedies which he had tried when he first felt its approach, and that he considered himself to be dangerously ill. "I am, however," he added, "prepared to die. Sit down on that block, and listen to what I shall say to you. Though I shall quit this state of being for another and a better, I confess that I was alarmed at the thought of expiring, before I had an opportunity of seeing and conversing with you. I am the depository of a secret, that I believe is known to no other living mortal. I once determined that it should die with me; and had I not met with you, it certainly should. But from our first acquaintance, my heart has been strongly attracted towards you; and as soon as I found you possessed of qualities to inspire esteem as well as regard, I felt disposed to give you this proof of my confidence. Still I hesitated. I first wished to deliberate on the probable effects of my disclosure upon the condition of society. I saw that it might produce evil, as well as good; but on weighing the two together, I have satisfied myself that the good will preponderate, and have determined to act accordingly. Take this key, (stretching out his feverish hand,) and after waiting two hours, in which time the medicine I have taken will have either produced a good effect, or put an end to my sufferings, you may then open that blue chest in the corner. It has a false bottom. On removing the paper which covers it, you will find the manuscript containing the important secret, together with some gold pieces, which I have saved for the day of need--because--(and he smiled in spite of his sufferings)--because hoarding is one of the pleasures of old men. Take them both, and use them discreetly. When I am gone, I request you, my friend, to discharge the last sad duties of humanity, and to see me buried according to the usages of my caste. The simple beings around me will then behold that I am mortal like themselves. And let this precious relic of female loveliness and worth, (taking a small picture, set in gold, from his bosom,) be buried with me. It has been warmed by my heart's blood for twenty-five years: let it be still near that heart when it ceases to beat. I have yet more to say to you; but my strength is too much exhausted."

The good old man here closed his eyes, with an expression of patient resignation, and rather as if he courted sleep than felt inclined to it: and, after shutting the door of his cell, I repaired to his little garden, to pass the allotted two hours. Left to my meditations, when I thought that I was probably about to be deprived for ever of the Hermit's conversation and society, I felt the wretchedness of my situation recur with all its former force. I sat down on a smooth rock under a tamarind tree, the scene of many an interesting conference between the Brahmin and myself; and I cast my eyes around--but how changed was every thing before me! I no longer regarded the sparkling eddies of the little cascade which fell down a steep rock at the upper end of the garden, and formed a pellucid basin below. The gay flowers and rich foliage of this genial climate--the bright plumage and cheerful notes of the birds--were all there; but my mind was not in a state to relish them. I arose, and in extreme agitation rambled over this little Eden, in which I had passed so many delightful hours.

Before the allotted time had elapsed--shall I confess it?--my fears for the Hermit were overcome by those that were purely selfish. It occurred to me, if he should thus suddenly die, and I be found alone in his cell, I might be charged with being his murderer; and my courage, which, from long inaction, had sadly declined of late, deserted me at the thought. After the most torturing suspense, the dial at length showed me that the two hours had elapsed, and I hastened to the cell.

I paused a moment at the door, afraid to enter, or even look in; made one or two steps, and hearing no sound, concluded that all was over with the Hermit, and that my own doom was sealed. My delight was inexpressible, therefore, when I perceived that he still breathed, and when, on drawing nearer, I found that he slept soundly. In a moment I passed from misery to bliss. I seated myself by his side, and there remained for more than an hour, enjoying the transition of my feelings. At length he awoke, and casting on me a look of placid benignity, said,--"Atterley, my time is not yet come. Though resigned to death, I am content to live. The worst is over. I am already almost restored to health." I then administered to him some refreshments, and, after a while, left him to repose. On again repairing to the garden, every object assumed its wonted appearance. The fragrance of the orange and the jasmine was no longer lost to me. The humming birds, which swarmed round the flowering cytisus and the beautiful water-fall, once more delighted the eye and the ear. I took my usual bath, as the sun was sinking below the mountain; and, finding the Hermit still soundly sleeping, I threw myself on a seat, under the shelter of some bamboos, fell asleep, and did not awake until late the next morning.

When I arose, I found the good Brahmin up, and, though much weakened by his disease, able to walk about. He told me that the Mirvoon, uneasy at my not returning as usual in the evening, had sent in search of me, and that the servant, finding me safe, was content to return without me. He advised me, however, not to repeat the same cause of alarm. Sing Fou, on hearing my explanation, readily forgave me for the uneasiness I had caused him. After a few days, the Brahmin recovered his ordinary health and strength; and having attended him at an earlier hour than usual, according to his request on the previous evening, he thus addressed me:--

"I have already told you, my dear Atterley, that I was born and educated at Benares, and that science is there more thoroughly understood and taught than the people of the west are aware of. We have, for many thousands of years, been good astronomers, chymists, mathematicians, and philosophers. We had discovered the secret of gunpowder, the magnetic attraction, the properties of electricity, long before they were heard of in Europe. We know more than we have revealed; and much of our knowledge is deposited in the archives of the caste to which I belong; but, for want of a language generally understood and easily learnt, (for these records are always written in the Sanscrit, that is no longer a spoken language,) and the diffusion which is given by the art of printing, these secrets of science are communicated only to a few, and sometimes even sleep with their authors, until a subsequent discovery, under more favourable circumstances, brings them again to light.

"It was at this seat of science that I learnt, from one of our sages, the physical truth which I am now about to communicate, and which he discovered, partly by his researches into the writings of ancient Pundits, and partly by his own extraordinary sagacity. There is a principle of repulsion as well as gravitation in the earth. It causes fire to rise upwards. It is exhibited in electricity. It occasions water-spouts, volcanoes, and earthquakes. After much labour and research, this principle has been found embodied in a metallic substance, which is met with in the mountain in which we are, united with a very heavy earth; and this circumstance had great influence in inducing me to settle myself here.

"This metal, when separated and purified, has as great a tendency to fly off from the earth, as a piece of gold or lead has to approach it. After making a number of curious experiments with it, we bethought ourselves of putting it to some use, and soon contrived, with the aid of it, to make cars and ascend into the air. We were very secret in these operations; for our unhappy country having then recently fallen under the subjection of the British nation, we apprehended that if we divulged our arcanum, they would not only fly away with all our treasures, whether found in palace or pagoda, but also carry off the inhabitants, to make them slaves in their colonies, as their government had not then abolished the African slave trade.

"After various trials and many successive improvements, in which our desires increased with our success, we determined to penetrate the aerial void as far as we could, providing for that purpose an apparatus, with which you will become better acquainted hereafter. In the course of our experiments, we discovered that this same metal, which was repelled from the earth, was in the same degree attracted towards the moon; for in one of our excursions, still aiming to ascend higher than we had ever done before, we were actually carried to that satellite; and if we had not there fallen into a lake, and our machine had not been water-tight, we must have been dashed to pieces or drowned. You will find in this book," he added, presenting me with a small volume, bound in green parchment, and fastened with silver clasps, "a minute detail of the apparatus to be provided, and the directions to be pursued in making this wonderful voyage. I have written it since I satisfied my mind that my fears of British rapacity were unfounded, and that I should do more good than harm by publishing the secret. But still I am not sure," he added, with one of his faint but significant smiles, "that I am not actuated by a wish to immortalize my name; for where is the mortal who would be indifferent to this object, if he thought he could attain it? Read the book at your leisure, and study it."

I listened to this recital with astonishment; and doubted at first, whether the Brahmin's late severe attack had not had the effect of unsettling his brain: but on looking in his face, the calm self-possession and intelligence which it exhibited, dispelled the momentary impression. I was all impatience to know the adventures he met with in the moon, asking him fifty questions in a breath, but was most anxious to learn if it had inhabitants, and what sort of beings they were.

"Yes," said he, "the moon has inhabitants, pretty much the same as the earth, of which they believe their globe to have been formerly a part. But suspend your questions, and let me give you a recital of the most remarkable things I saw there."

I checked my impatience, and listened with all my ears to the wonders he related. He went on to inform me that the inhabitants of the moon resembled those of the earth, in form, stature, features, and manners, and were evidently of the same species, as they did not differ more than did the Hottentot from the Parisian. That they had similar passions, propensities, and pursuits, but differed greatly in manners and habits. They had more activity, but less strength: they were feebler in mind as well as body. But the most curious part of his information was, that a large number of them were born without any intellectual vigour, and wandered about as so many automatons, under the care of the government, until they were illuminated with the mental ray from some earthly brains, by means of the mysterious influence which the moon is known to exercise on our planet. But in this case the inhabitant of the earth loses what the inhabitant of the moon gains--the ordinary portion of understanding allotted to one mortal being thus divided between two; and, as might be expected, seeing that the two minds were originally the same, there is a most exact conformity between the man of the earth and his counterpart in the moon, in all their principles of action and modes of thinking.

These Glonglims, as they are called, after they have been thus imbued with intellect, are held in peculiar respect by the vulgar, and are thought to be in every way superior to those whose understandings are entire. The laws by which two objects, so far apart, operate on each other, have been, as yet, but imperfectly developed, and the wilder their freaks, the more they are the objects of wonder and admiration. "The science of *lunarology*," he observed, "is yet in its infancy. But in the three voyages I have made to the moon, I have acquired so many new facts, and imparted so many to the learned men of that planet, that it is, without doubt, the subject of their active speculations at this time, and will, probably, assume a regular form long before the new science of phrenology of which you tell me, and which it must, in time, supersede. Now and then, though very rarely, the man of the earth regains the intellect he has lost; in which case his lunar counterpart returns to his former state of imbecility. Both parties are entirely unconscious of the change--one, of what he has lost, and the other of what he has gained."

The Brahmin then added: "Though our party are the only voyagers of which authentic history affords any testimony, yet it is probable, from obscure hints in some of our most ancient writings in the Sanscrit, that the voyage has been made in remote periods of antiquity; and the Lunarians have a similar tradition. While, in the revolutions which have so changed the affairs of mankind on our globe, (and probably in its satellite,) the art has been lost, faint traces of its existence may be perceived in the opinions of the vulgar, and in many of their ordinary forms of expression. Thus it is generally believed throughout all Asia, that the moon has an influence on the brain; and when a man is of insane mind, we call him a lunatic. One of the curses of the common people is, 'May the moon eat up your brains;' and in China they say of a man who has done any act of egregious folly, 'He was gathering wool in the moon.'"

I was struck with these remarks, and told the Hermit that the language of Europe afforded the same indirect evidence of the fact he mentioned: that my own language especially, abounded with expressions which could be explained on no other hypothesis;--for, besides the terms "lunacy," "lunatic," and the supposed influence of the moon on the brain, when we see symptoms of a disordered intellect, we say the mind *wanders*, which evidently alludes to a part of it rambling to a distant region, as is the moon. We say too, a man is "out of his head," that is, his mind being in another man's head, must of course be out of his own. To "know no more than the man in the moon," is a proverbial expression for ignorance, and is without meaning, unless it be considered to refer to the Glonglims. We say that an insane man is "distracted;" by which we mean that his mind is drawn two different ways. So also, we call a lunatic *a man beside himself*, which most distinctly expresses the two distinct bodies his mind now animates. There are, moreover, many other analogous expressions, as "moonstruck," "deranged," "extravagant," and some others, which, altogether, form a mass of concurring testimony that it is impossible to resist.

"Be that as it may," said he, "whether the voyage has been made in former times or not, is of little importance: it is sufficient for us to know that it has been effected in our time, and can be effected again. I am anxious to repeat the voyage, for the purpose of ascertaining some facts, about which I have been lately speculating; and I wish, besides, to afford you ocular demonstration of the wonders I have disclosed; for, in spite of your good opinion of my veracity, I have sometimes perceived symptoms of incredulity about you, and I do not wonder at it."

The love of the marvellous, and the wish for a change, which had long slumbered in my bosom, were now suddenly awakened, and I eagerly caught at his proposal.

"When can we set out, father?" said I.

"Not so fast," replied he; "we have a great deal of preparation to make. Our apparatus requires the best workmanship, and we cannot here command either first-rate articles or materials, without incurring the risk of suspicion and interruption. While most of the simple villagers are kindly disposed towards me, there are a few who regard me with distrust and malevolence, and would readily avail themselves of an opportunity to bring me under the censure of the priesthood and the government. Besides, the governor of Mergui would probably be glad to lay hold of any plausible evidence against you, as affording him the best chance of avoiding any future reckoning either with you or his superiors. We must therefore be very secret in our plans. I know an ingenious artificer in copper and other metals, whose only child I was instrumental in curing of scrofula, and in whose fidelity, as well as good will, I can safely rely. But we must give him time. He can construct our machine at home, and we must take our departure from that place in the night."

CHAPTER III.

The Brahmin and Atterley prepare for their voyage--Description of their machine--Incidents of the voyage--The appearance of the earth; Africa; Greece--The Brahmin's speculations on the different races of men--National character.

Having thus formed our plan of operations, we the next day proceeded to put them in execution. The coppersmith agreed to undertake the work we wanted done, for a moderate compensation; but we did not think it prudent to inform him of our object, which he supposed was to make some philosophical experiment. It was forthwith arranged that he should occasionally visit the Hermit, to receive instructions, as if for the purpose of asking medical advice. During this interval my mind was absorbed with our project; and when in company, I was so thoughtful and abstracted, that it has since seemed strange to me that Sing Fou's suspicions that I was planning my escape were not more excited. At length, by dint of great exertion, in about three months every thing was in readiness, and we determined on the following night to set out on our perilous expedition.

The machine in which we proposed to embark, was a copper vessel, that would have been an exact cube of six feet, if the corners and edges had not been rounded off. It had an opening large enough to receive our bodies, which was closed by double sliding pannels, with quilted cloth between them. When these were properly adjusted, the machine was perfectly air-tight, and strong enough, by means of iron bars running alternately inside and out, to resist the pressure of the atmosphere, when the machine should be exhausted of its air, as we took the precaution to prove by the aid of an air-pump. On the top of the copper chest and on the outside, we had as much of the lunar metal (which I shall henceforth call ***lunarium***) as we found, by calculation and experiment, would overcome the weight of the machine, as well as its contents, and take us to the moon on the third day. As the air which the machine contained, would not be sufficient for our respiration more than about six hours, and the chief part of the space we were to pass through was a mere void, we provided ourselves with a sufficient supply, by condensing it in a small globular vessel, made partly of iron and partly of lunarium, to take off its weight. On my return, I gave Mr. Jacob Perkins, who is now in England, a hint of this plan of condensation, and it has there obtained him great celebrity. This fact I should not have thought it worth while to mention, had he not taken the sole merit of the invention to himself; at least I cannot hear that in his numerous public notices he has ever mentioned my name.

But to return. A small circular window, made of a single piece of thick clear glass, was neatly fitted on each of the six sides. Several pieces of lead were securely fastened to screws which passed through the bottom of the machine; as well as a thick plank. The screws were so contrived, that by turning them in one direction, the pieces of lead attached to them were immediately disengaged from the hooks with which they were connected. The pieces of lunarium were fastened in like manner to screws, which passed through the top of the machine; so that by turning them in one direction, those metallic pieces would fly into the air with the velocity of a rocket. The Brahmin took with him a thermometer, two telescopes, one of which projected through the top of the machine, and the other through the bottom; a phosphoric lamp, pen, ink, and paper, and some light refreshments sufficient to supply us for some days.

The moon was then in her third quarter, and near the zenith: it was, of course, a little after midnight, and when the coppersmith and his family were in their soundest sleep, that we entered the machine. In about an hour more we had the doors secured, and every thing arranged in its place, when, cutting the cords which fastened us to the ground, by means of small steel blades which worked in the ends of other screws, we rose from the earth with a whizzing sound, and a sensation at first of very rapid ascent: but after a short time, we were scarcely sensible of any motion in the machine, except when we changed our places.

The ardent curiosity I had felt to behold the wonderful things which the Brahmin related, and the hope of returning soon to my children and native country, had made me most impatient for the moment of departure; during which time the hazards and difficulties of the voyage were entirely overlooked: but now that the moment of execution had arrived, and I found myself shut up in this small chest, and about to enter on a voyage so new, so strange, and beset with such a variety of dangers, I will not deny that my courage failed me, and I would gladly have compromised to return to Mozaun, and remain there quietly all the rest of my days. But shame restrained me, and I dissembled my emotions.

At our first shock on leaving the earth, my fears were at their height; but after about two hours, I had tolerably well regained my composure, to which the returning light of day greatly contributed. By this time we had a full view of the rising sun, pouring a flood of light over one half of the circular landscape below us, and leaving the rest in shade. While those natural objects, the rivers and mountains, land and sea, were fast receding from our view, our horizon kept gradually extending as we mounted: but ere 10 o'clock this effect ceased, and the broad disc of the earth began sensibly to diminish.

It is impossible to describe my sensations of mingled awe and admiration at the splendid spectacle beneath me, so long as the different portions of the earth's surface were plainly distinguishable. The novelty of the situation in which I found myself, as well as its danger, prevented me indeed at first from giving more than a passing attention to the magnificent scene; but after a while, encouraged by the Brahmin's exhortation, and yet more by the example of his calm and assured air, I was able to take a more leisurely view of it. At first, as we partook of the diurnal motion of the earth, and our course was consequently oblique, the same portion of the globe from which we had set out, continued directly under us; and as the eye stretched in every direction over Asia and its seas, continents and islands, they appeared like pieces of green velvet, the surrounding ocean like a mirror, and the Ganges, the Hoogley, and the great rivers of China, like threads of silver.

About 11 o'clock it was necessary to get a fresh supply of air, when my companion cautiously turned one of the two stop-cocks to let out that which was no longer fit for respiration, requesting me, at the same time, to turn the other, to let in a fresh supply of condensed air; but being awkward in the first attempt to follow his directions, I was so affected by the exhaustion of the air through the vent now made for it, that I fainted; and having, at the same time, given freer passage to the condensed air than I ought, we must in a few seconds have lost our supply, and thus have inevitably perished, had not the watchful Hermit seen the mischief, and repaired it almost as soon as it occurred. This accident, and the various agitations my mind had undergone in the course of the day, so overpowered me, that at an early hour in the afternoon I fell into a profound sleep, and did not awake again for eight hours.

While I slept, the good Brahmin had contrived to manage both stop-cocks himself. The time of my waking would have been about 11 o'clock at night, if we had continued on the earth; but we were now in a region where there was no alternation of day and night, but one unvarying cloudless sun. Its heat, however, was not in proportion to its brightness; for we found that after we had ascended a few miles from the earth, it was becoming much colder, and the Brahmin had recourse to a chemical process for evolving heat, which soon made us comfortable: but after we were fairly in the great aerial void, the temperature of our machine showed no tendency to change.

The sensations caused by the novelty of my situation, at first checked those lively and varied trains of thought which the bird's-eye view of so many countries passing in review before us, was calculated to excite: yet, after I had become more familiar with it, I contemplated the beautiful exhibition with inexpressible delight. Besides, a glass of cordial, as well as the calm, confiding air of the Brahmin, contributed to restore me to my self-possession. The reader will recollect, that although our motion, at first, partook of that of the earth's on its axis, and although the *positive* effect was the same on our course, the *relative* effect was less and less as we ascended, and consequently, that after a certain height, every part of the terraqueous globe would present itself to our view in succession, as we rapidly receded from it. At 9 o'clock, the whole of India was a little to the west of us, and we saw, as in a map, that fertile and populous region, which has been so strangely reduced to subjection, by a company of merchants belonging to a country on the opposite side of the globe--a country not equal to one-fourth of it, in extent or population. Its rivers were like small filaments of silver; the Red Sea resembled a narrow plate of the same metal. The peninsula of India was of a darker, and Arabia of a light and more grayish green.

The sun's rays striking obliquely on the Atlantic, emitted an effulgence that was dazzling to the eyes. For two or three hours the appearance of the earth did not greatly vary, the wider extent of surface we could survey, compensating for our greater distance; and indeed at that time we could not see the whole horizon, without putting our eyes close to the glass.

When the Brahmin saw that I had overcome my first surprise, and had acquired somewhat of his own composure, he manifested a disposition to beguile the time with conversation. "Look through the telescope," said he, "a little from the sun, and observe the continent of Africa, which is presenting itself to our view." I took a hasty glance over it, and perceived that its northern edge was fringed with green; then a dull white belt marked the great Sahara, or Desert, and then it exhibited a deep green again, to its most southern extremity. I tried in vain to discover the pyramids, for our telescope had not sufficient power to show them.

I observed to him, that less was known of this continent than of the others: that a spirit of lively curiosity had been excited by the western nations of Europe, to become acquainted with the inhabited parts of the globe; but that all the efforts yet made, had still left a large portion almost entirely unknown. I asked if he did not think it probable that some of the nations in the interior of Africa were more advanced in civilization than those on the coast, whose barbarous custom of making slaves of their prisoners, Europeans had encouraged and perpetuated, by purchasing them.

"No, no," said he; "the benefits of civilization could not have been so easily confined, but would have spread themselves over every part of that continent, or at least as far as the Great Desert, if they had ever existed. The intense heat of a climate, lying on each side of the Line, at once disinclines men to exertion, and renders it unnecessary. Vegetable diet is more suited to them than animal, which favours a denser population. Talent is elicited by the efforts required to overcome difficulties and hardships; and their natural birth-place is a country of frost and snow--of tempests--of sterility enough to give a spur to exertion, but not enough to extinguish hope. Where these difficulties exist, and give occasion to war and emulation, the powers of the human mind are most frequently developed."

"Do you think then," said I, "that there is no such thing as natural inferiority and differences of races?"

"I have been much perplexed by that question," said he. "When I regard the great masses of mankind, I think there seems to be among them some characteristic differences. I see that the Europeans have every where obtained the ascendancy over those who inhabit the other quarters of the globe. But when I compare individuals, I see always the same passions, the same motives, the same mental operations; and my opinion is changed. The same seed becomes a very different plant when sowed in one soil or another, and put under this or that mode of cultivation."

"And may not," said I, "the very nature of the plant be changed, after a long continuance of the same culture in the same soil?"

"Why, that is but another mode of stating the question. I rather think, if it has generally degenerated, it may, by opposite treatment, be also gradually brought back to its original excellence."

"Who knows, then," said I, "what our missionaries and colonization societies may effect in Africa."

He inquired of me what these societies were; and on explaining their history, observed: "By what you tell me, it is indeed a small beginning; but if they can get this grain of mustard-seed to grow, there is no saying how much it may multiply. See what a handful of colonists have done in your own country. A few ship-loads of English have overspread half a continent; and, from what you tell me, their descendants will amount, in another century, to more than one hundred millions. There is no rule," he continued, "that can be laid down on this subject, to which some nations cannot be found to furnish a striking exception. If mere difficulties were all that were wanting to call forth the intellectual energies of man, they have their full share on the borders of the Great Desert. There are in that whitish tract which separates the countries on the southern shores of the Mediterranean from the rest of Africa, thousands of human beings at this moment toiling over that dreary ocean of sand, to whom a draught of fresh water would be a blessing, and the simplest meal a luxury.

"Perhaps, however, you will say they are so engrossed with the animal wants of hunger and thirst, that they are incapable of attending to any thing else. Be it so. But in the interior they are placed in parallel circumstances with the natives of Europe: they are engaged in struggles for territory and dominion--for their altars and their homes; and this state of things, which has made some of them brave and warlike, has made none poets or painters, historians or philosophers. There, poetry has not wanted themes of great achievement and noble daring; but heroes have wanted poets. Nor can we justly ascribe the difference to the enervating influence of climate, for the temperature of the most southern parts of Africa differs little from that of Greece. And the tropical nations, too, of your own continent, the Peruvians, were more improved than those who inhabited the temperate regions. Besides, though the climate had instilled softness and feebleness of character, it might also have permitted the cultivation of the arts, as has been the case with us in Asia. On the whole, without our being able to pronounce with certainty on the subject, it does seem probable that some organic difference exists in the various races of mankind, to which their diversities of moral and intellectual character may in part be referred."--By this time the Morea and the Grecian Archipelago were directly under our telescope.

"Does not Greece," said I, "furnish the clearest proof of the influence of moral causes on the character of nations? Compare what that country formerly was, with what it now is. Once superior to all the rest of the habitable globe, (of which it did not constitute the thousandth part,) in letters, arts, and arms, and all that distinguishes men from brutes; not merely in their own estimation, (for all nations are disposed to rate themselves high enough,) but by the general consent of the rest of the world. Do not the most improved and civilized of modern states still take them as their instructors and guides in every species of literature--in philosophy, history, oratory, poetry, architecture, and sculpture? And those too, who have attained superiority over the world, in arms, yield a voluntary subjection to the Greeks in the arts. The cause of their former excellence and their present inferiority, is no doubt to be found in their former freedom and their present slavery, and in the loss of that emulation which seems indispensable to natural greatness."

"Nay," replied he, "I am very far from denying the influence of moral causes on national character. The history of every country affords abundant evidence of it. I mean only to say, that though it does much, it does not do every thing. It seems more reasonable to impute the changes in national character to the mutable habits and institutions of man, than to nature, which is always the same. But if we look a little nearer, we may perhaps perceive, that amidst all those mutations in the character of nations, there are still some features that are common to the same people at all times, and which it would therefore be reasonable to impute to the great un-varying laws of nature. Thus it requires no extraordinary acuteness of observation, no strained hypothesis, to perceive a close resemblance between the Germans or the Britons of antiquity and their modern descendants, after the lapse of eighteen centuries, and an entire revolution in government, religion, language, and laws. And travellers still perceive among the inhabitants of modern Greece, deteriorat-ed and debased as they are by political servitude, many of those qualities which distinguished their predecessors: the same natural acuteness--the same sensibility to pleasure--the same pliancy of mind and elasticity of body--the same aptitude for the arts of imitation--and the same striking physiognomy. That bright, serene sky--that happy combination of land and water, constituting the perfection of the picturesque, and that balmy softness of its air, which have proved themselves so propitious to forms of beauty, agility, and strength, also operate benignantly on the mind which animates them. Whilst the fruit is still fair to the eye, it is not probable that it has permanently degenerated in fragrance or flavour. The great diversities of national character may, perhaps, be attributed principally to moral and accidental causes, but partly also to climate, and to original diversities in the different races of man."

CHAPTER IV.

Continuation of the voyage--View of Europe; Atlantic Ocean; America--
Speculations on the future destiny of the United States--Moral reflections
--Pacific Ocean--Hypothesis on the origin of the Moon.

By this time the whole Mediterranean Sea, which, with the Arabian Gulf, was seen to separate Africa from Europe and Asia, was full in our view. The political divisions of these quarters of the world were, of course, undistinguishable; and few of the natural were discernible by the naked eye. The Alps were marked by a white streak, though less bright than the water. By the aid of our glass, we could just discern the Danube, the Nile, and a river which empties itself into the Gulf of Guinea, and which I took to be the Niger: but the other streams were not perceptible. The most conspicuous object of the solid part of the globe, was the Great Desert before mentioned. The whole of Africa, indeed, was of a lighter hue than either Asia or Europe, owing, I presume, to its having a greater proportion of sandy soil: and I could not avoid contrasting, in my mind, the colour of these continents, as they now appeared, with the complexions of their respective inhabitants.

I was struck too, with the vast disproportion which the extent of the several countries of the earth bore to the part they had acted in history, and the influence they had exerted on human affairs. The British islands had diminished to a speck, and France was little larger; yet, a few years ago it seemed, at least to us in the United States, as if there were no other nations on the earth. The Brahmin, who was well read in European history, on my making a remark on this subject, reminded me that Athens and Sparta had once obtained almost equal celebrity, although they were so small as not now to be visible. As I slowly passed the telescope over the face of Europe, I pictured to myself the fat, plodding Hollander--the patient, contemplative German--the ingenious, sensual Italian--the temperate Swiss--the haughty, superstitious Spaniard--the sprightly, self-complacent Frenchman--the sullen and reflecting Englishman --who monopolize nearly all the science and literature of the earth, to which they bear so small a proportion. As the Atlantic fell under our view, two faint circles on each side of the equator, were to be perceived by the naked eye. They were less bright than the rest of the ocean. The Brahmin suggested that they might be currents; which brought to my memory Dr. Franklin's conjecture on the subject, now completely verified by this circular line of vapour, as it had been previously rendered probable by the floating substances, which had been occasionally picked up, at great distances from the places where they had been thrown into the ocean. The circle was whiter and more distinct, where the Gulf Stream runs parallel to the American coast, and gradually grew fainter as it passed along the Banks of Newfoundland, to the coast of Europe, where, taking a southerly direction, the line of the circle was barely discernible. A similar circle of vapour, though less defined and complete, was perceived in the South Atlantic Ocean.

When the coast of my own beloved country first presented itself to my view, I experienced the liveliest emotions; and I felt so anxious to see my children and friends, that I would gladly have given up all the promised pleasures of our expedition. I even ventured to hint my feelings to the Brahmin; but he, gently rebuking my impatience, said--

"If to return home had been your only object, and not to see what not one of your nation or race has ever yet seen, you ought to have so informed me, that we might have arranged matters accordingly. I do not wish you to return to your country, until you will be enabled to make yourself welcome and useful there, by what you may see in the lunar world. Take courage, then, my friend; you have passed the worst; and, as the proverb says, do not, when you have swallowed the ox, now choke at the tail. Besides, although we made all possible haste in descending, we should, ere we reached the surface, find ourselves to the west of your continent, and be compelled then to choose between some part of Asia or the Pacific Ocean."

"Let us then proceed," said I, mortified at the imputation on my courage, and influenced yet more, perhaps, by the last argument. The Brahmin then tried to soothe my disappointment, by his remarks on my native land.

"I have a great curiosity," said he, "to see a country where a man, by his labour, can earn as much in a month as will procure him bread, and meat too, for the whole year; in a week, as will pay his dues to the government; and in one or two days, as will buy him an acre of good land: where every man preaches whatever religion he pleases; where the priests of the different sects never fight, and seldom quarrel; and, stranger than all, where the authority of government derives no aid from an army, and that of the priests no support from the law."

I told him, when he should see these things in operation with his own eyes, as I trusted he would, if it pleased heaven to favour our undertakings, they would appear less strange. I reminded him of the peculiar circumstances under which our countrymen had commenced their career.

"In all other countries," said I, "civilization and population have gone hand in hand; and the necessity of an increasing subsistence for increasing numbers, has been the parent of useful arts and of social improvement. In every successive stage of their advancement, such countries have equally felt the evils occasioned by a scanty and precarious subsistence. In America, however, the people are in the full enjoyment of all the arts of civilization, while they are unrestricted in their means of subsistence, and consequently in their power of multiplication. From this singular state of things, two consequences result. One is, that the progress of the nation in wealth, power, and greatness, is more rapid than the world has ever before witnessed. Another is, that our people, being less cramped and fettered by their necessities, and feeling, of course, less of those moral evils which poverty and discomfort engender, their character, moral and intellectual, will be developed and matured with greater celerity, and, I incline to think, carried to a higher point of excellence than has ever yet been attained. I anticipate for them the eloquence and art of Athens--the courage and love of country of Sparta--the constancy and military prowess of the Romans--the science and literature of England and France--the industry of the Dutch--the temperance and obedience to the laws of the Swiss. In fifty years, their numbers will amount to forty millions; in a century, to one hundred and sixty millions; in two centuries, (allowing for a decreasing rate of multiplication,) to three or four hundred millions. Nor does it seem impossible that, from the structure of their government, they may continue united for a few great national purposes, while each State may make the laws that are suited to its peculiar habits, character, and circumstances. In another half century, they will extend the Christian religion and the English language to the Pacific Ocean.

"To the south of them, on the same continent, other great nations will arise, who, if they were to be equally united, might contend in terrible conflicts for the mastery of this great continent, and even of the world. But when they shall be completely liberated from the yoke of Spanish dominion, and have for some time enjoyed that full possession of their faculties and energies which liberty only can give, they will probably split into distinct States. United, at first, by the sympathy of men struggling in the same cause, and by similarity of manners and religion, they will, after a while, do as men always have done, quarrel and fight; and these wars will check their social improvement, and mar their political hopes. Whether they will successively fall under the dominion of one able and fortunate leader, or, like the motley sovereignties of Europe, preserve their integrity by their mutual jealousy, time only can show."

"Your reasoning about the natives of Spanish America appears very probable," said the Brahmin; "but is it not equally applicable to your own country ?"

I reminded him of the peculiar advantages of our government. He shook his head.

"No, Atterley," said he, "do not deceive yourself. The duration of every species of polity is uncertain; the works of nature alone are permanent. The motions of the heavenly bodies are the same as they were thousands of years ago. But not so with the works of man. He is the identical animal that he ever was. His political institutions, however cunningly devised, have always been yet more perishable than his structures of stone and marble. This is according to all past history: and do not, therefore, count upon an exception in your favour, that would be little short of the miraculous. But," he good-naturedly added, "such a miracle may take place in your system; and, although I do not expect it, I sincerely wish it."

We were now able to see one half of the broad expanse of the Pacific, which glistened with the brightness of quicksilver or polished steel.

"Cast your eyes to the north," said he, "and see where your continent and mine approach so near as almost to touch. Both these coasts are at this time thinly inhabited by a rude and miserable people, whose whole time is spent in struggling against the rigours of their dreary climate, and the scantiness of its productions. Yet, perhaps the Indians and the Kamtschadales will be gradually moulded into a hardy, civilized people: and here may be the scene of many a fierce conflict between your people and the Russians, whose numbers, now four times as great as yours, increase almost as rapidly."

He then amused me with accounts of the manners and mode of life of the Hyperborean race, with whom he had once passed a summer. Glancing my eye then to the south,--"See," said I, "while the Kamtschadale is providing his supply of furs and of fish, for the long winter which is already knocking at the door of his hut, the gay and voluptuous native of the Sandwich and other islands between the tropics. How striking the contrast! The one passes his life in ease, abundance, and enjoyment; the other in toil, privation, and care. No inclemency of the seasons inflicts present suffering on these happy islanders, or brings apprehensions for the future. Nature presents them with her most delicious fruits spontaneously and abundantly; and she has implanted in their breast a lively relish for the favours she so lavishly bestows upon them."

The Brahmin, after musing a while, replied: "The difference is far less than you imagine. Perhaps, on balancing their respective pleasures and pains, the superior gain of the islander will be reduced to nothing: for, as to the simplest source of gratification, that of palatable food, if nature produces it more liberally in the islands, she also produces there more mouths to consume it. The richest Kamtschadale may, indeed, oftener go without a dinner than the richest Otaheitan; but it may be quite the reverse with the poorest. Then, as to quality of the food: if nature has provided more delicious fruits for the natives of tropical climates, she has given a sharper appetite and stronger digestion to the Hyperborean, which equalizes the sum of their enjoyments. A dry crust is relished, when an individual is hungry, more than the most savoury and delicate dainties when he is in a fever; and water to one man, is a more delicious beverage than the juice of the grape or of the palm to another. As to the necessity for labour, which is ever pressing on the inhabitants of cold countries, it is this consequent and incessant activity which gives health to their bodies, and cheerful vigour to their minds; since, without such exercise, man would have been ever a prey to disease and discontent. And, if no other occupation be provided for the mind of man, it carves out employment for itself in vain regrets and gloomy forebodings--in jealousy, envy, and the indulgence of every hateful and tormenting passion: hence the proverb,--'If you want corn, cultivate your soil; if you want weeds, let it alone.'

"But again: the native of those sunny isles is never sensible of the bounty of Providence, till he is deprived of it. Here, as well as every where else, desire outgoes gratification. Man sees or fancies much that he cannot obtain; and in his regret for what he wants, forgets what he already possesses. What is it to one with a tooth-ache, that a savoury dish is placed before him? It is the same with the mind as the body: when pain engrosses it in one way, it cannot relish pleasure in another. Every climate and country too, have their own evils and inconveniences."

"You think, then," said I, "that the native of Kamtschatka has the advantage?"

"No," he rejoined, "I do not mean to say that, for the evils of his situation are likewise very great; but they are more manifest, and therefore less necessary to be brought to your notice."

It was now, by our time-pieces, about two o'clock in the afternoon--that is, two hours had elapsed since we left terra firma; and, saving a few biscuits and a glass of cordial a-piece, we had not taken any sort of refreshment. The Brahmin proposed that we now should dine; and, opening a small case, and drawing forth a cold fowl, a piece of dried goat's flesh, a small pot of ghee, some biscuits, and a bottle of arrack flavoured with ginger and spices, with a larger one of water, we ate as heartily as we had ever done at the hermitage; the slight motion of our machine to one side or the other, whenever we moved, giving us nearly as much exercise as a vessel in a smooth sea. The animal food had been provided for me, for the Brahmin satisfied his hunger with the ghee, sweetmeats, and biscuit, and ate sparingly even of them. We each took two glasses of the cordial diluted with water, and carefully putting back the fragments, again turned our thoughts to the planet we had left.

The middle of the Pacific now lay immediately beneath us. I had never before been struck with the irregular distribution of land and water on our globe, the expanse of ocean here being twice as large as in any other part; and, on remarking this striking difference to the Brahmin, he replied:

"It is the opinion of some philosophers in the moon, that their globe is a fragment of ours; and, as they can see every part of the earth's surface, they believe the Pacific was the place from which the moon was ejected. They pretend that a short, but consistent tradition of the disruption, has regularly been transmitted from remote antiquity; and they draw confirmation of their hypothesis from many words of the Chinese, and other Orientals, with whom they claim affinity."

"Ridiculous!" said I; "the moon is one-fourth the diameter of the earth; and if the two were united in one sphere, the highest mountains must have been submerged, and of course there would have been no human inhabitants; or, if any part of the land was then bare, on the waters retiring to fill up the chasm made by the separation of so large a body as the moon, the parts before habitable would be, instead of two, three, or at most four miles, as your Himalah mountains are said to be, some twenty or thirty miles above the level of the ocean."

"That is not quite so certain," said he: "we know not of what the interior of the earth is composed, any more than we could distinguish the contents of an egg, by penetrating one hundredth part of its shell. But we see, that if one drop of water be united with another, they form one large drop, as spherical as either of the two which composed it: and on the separation of the moon from the earth, if they were composed of mingled solids and fluids, or if the solid parts rested on fluid, both the fragment and the remaining earth would assume the same globular appearance they now present.

"On this subject, however, I give no opinion. I only say, that it is not contradicted by the facts you have mentioned. The fluid and the solid parts settling down into a new sphere, might still retain nearly their former proportion: or, if the fragment took away a greater proportion of solid than of fluid, then the waters retiring to fill up the cavity, would leave parts bare which they had formerly covered. There are some facts which give a colour to this supposition; for most of the high mountains of the earth afford evidence of former submersion; and those which are the highest, the Himalah, are situated in the country to which the origin of civilization, and even the human species itself, may be traced. The moon too, we know, has much less water than the earth: and all those appearances of violence, which have so puzzled cosmogonists, the topsy-turvy position in which vegetable substances are occasionally found beneath the soil on which they grew, and the clear manifestations of the action of water, in the formation of strata, in the undulating forms it has left, and in the correspondent salient and retiring angles of mountains and opposite coasts, were all caused by the disruption; and as the moon has a smaller proportion of water than the earth, she has also the highest mountains."

"But, father," said I, "the diameter of the earth being but four times as large as that of the moon, how can the violent separation of so large a portion of our planet be accounted for? Where is the mighty agent to rend off such a mass, and throw it to thirty times the earth's diameter?"

"Upon that subject," said he, "the Lunarian sages are much divided. Many hypotheses have been suggested on the subject, some of which are very ingenious, and all very fanciful: but the two most celebrated, and into which all the others are now merged, are those of Neerlego and Darcandarca; the former of whom, in a treatise extending to nine quarto volumes, has maintained that the disruption was caused by a comet; and the latter, in a work yet more voluminous, has endeavoured to prove, that when the materials of the moon composed a part of the earth, this planet contained large masses of water, which, though the particles cohered with each other, were disposed to fly off from the earth; and that, by an accumulation of the electric fluid, according to laws which he has attempted to explain, the force was at length sufficient to heave the rocks which encompassed these masses, from their beds, and to project them from the earth, when, partaking of the earth's diurnal motion, they assumed a spherical form, and revolved around it. And further, that because the moon is composed of two sorts of matter, that are differently affected towards the earth in its revolution round that planet, the same parts of its surface always maintain some relative position to us, which thus necessarily causes the singularity of her turning on her axis precisely in the time in which she revolves round the earth."

"I see," said I, "that doctors differ and dispute about their own fancies every where."

"That is," said he, "because they contend as vehemently for what they imagine as for what they see; and perhaps more so, as their *perceptions* are like those of other men, while their *reveries* are more exclusively their own. Thus, in the present instance, the controversy turns upon the mode in which the separation was effected, which affords the widest field for conjecture, while they both agree that such separation has taken place. As to this fact I have not yet made up my mind, though it must be confessed that there is much to give plausibility to their opinion. I recognise, for instance, a striking resemblance between the animal and vegetable productions of Asia and those of the moon."

"Do you think, father," said I, "that animal, or even vegetable life, could possibly exist in such a disruption as is supposed?"

"Why not?" said he: "you are not to imagine that the shock would be felt in proportion to the mass that was moved. On the contrary, while it would occasion, in some parts, a great destruction of life, it would, in others, not be felt more than an earthquake, or rather, than a succession of earthquakes, during the time that the different parts of the mass were adjusting themselves to a spherical form; whilst a few pairs, or even a single pair of animals, saved in some cavity of a mountain, would be sufficient, in a few centuries, to stock the whole surface of the earth with as many individuals as are now to be found on it.

"After all," he added, "it is often difficult in science to distinguish Truth from the plausibility which personates her. But let us not, however, be precipitate; let us but hear both sides. In the east we have a saying, that 'he who hears with but one ear, never hears well.'"

CHAPTER V.

The voyage continued--Second view of Asia--The Brahmin's speculations concerning India--Increase of the Moon's attraction--Appearance of the Moon--They land on the Moon.

The dryness of the preceding discussion, which lay out of the course of my studies, together with the effect of my dinner, began to make me a little drowsy; whereupon the Brahmin urged me to take the repose which it was clear I needed; remarking, that when I awoke, he would follow my example. Reclining my head, then, on my cloak, in a few minutes my senses were steeped in forgetfulness.

I slept about six hours most profoundly; and on waking, found the good Brahmin busy with his calculations of our progress. I insisted on his now taking some rest. After requesting me to wake him at the end of three hours, (or sooner, if any thing of moment should occur,) and putting up a short prayer, which was manifested by his looks, rather than by his words, he laid himself down, and soon fell into a quiet sleep.

Left now to my own meditations, and unsupported by the example and conversation of my friend, I felt my first apprehensions return, and began seriously to regret my rashness in thus venturing on so bold an experiment, which, however often repeated with success, must ever be hazardous, and which could plead little more in its favour than a vain and childish curiosity. I took up a book, but whilst my eye ran over the page, I understood but little what I read, and could not relish even that. I now looked down through the telescope, and found the earth surprisingly diminished in her apparent dimensions, from the increased rapidity of our ascent. The eastern coasts of Asia were still fully in view, as well as the entire figure of that vast continent--of New Holland--of Ceylon, and of Borneo; but the smaller islands were invisible. I strained my eye to no purpose, to follow the indentations of the coast, according to the map before me; the great bays and promontories could alone be perceived. The Burman Empire, in one of the insignificant villages of which I had been confined for a few years, was now reduced to a speck. The agreeable hours I had passed with the Brahmin, with the little daughter of Sing Fou, and my rambling over the neighbouring heights, all recurred to my mind, and I almost regretted the pleasures I had relinquished. I tried, with more success, to beguile the time by making notes in my journal; and after having devoted about an hour to this object, I returned to the telescope, and now took occasion to examine the figure of the earth near the Poles, with a view of discovering whether its form favoured Captain Symmes's theory of an aperture existing there; and I am convinced that that ingenious gentleman is mistaken. Time passed so heavily during these solitary occupations, that I looked at my watch every five minutes, and could scarcely be persuaded it was not out of order. I then took up my little Bible, (which had always been my travelling companion,) read a few chapters in St. Matthew, and found my feelings tranquillized, and my courage increased. The desired hour at length arrived; when, on waking the old man, he alertly raised himself up, and at the first view of the diminished appearance of the earth, observed that our journey was a third over, as to time, but not as to distance. After a few moments, the Brahmin again cast his eye towards his own natal soil; on beholding which, he fetched a deep sigh, and, if I was not mistaken, I saw a rising tear.

"Alas!" said he, "my country and my countrymen, how different you are in many respects from what I should wish you to be! And yet I do not love you the less. Perhaps I love you the more for your faults, as well as for your misfortunes.

"Our lot," continued he, "is a hard one. That quarter of the world has sent letters, and arts, and religion abroad to adorn and benefit the other four; and these, the chief of human blessings and glories, have deserted us!"

I told him that I had heard the honours, which he claimed for India, attributed to Egypt. He contended, with true love of country, great plausibility, and an intimate knowledge of Oriental history, that letters and the arts had been first transplanted from Asia into Egypt.

"No other part of Africa," said he, "saving Egypt, can boast of any ancient monuments of the arts or of civilization. Even the pyramids, the great boast of Egypt, are proofs of nothing more than ordinary patient labour, directed by despotic power. Besides, look at that vast region, extending five thousand miles from the Mediterranean to the Cape of Good Hope, and four thousand from the Red Sea to the Atlantic. Its immense surface contains only ignorant barbarians, who are as uncivilized now as they were three thousand years ago. Is it likely that if civilization and letters originated in Egypt, as is sometimes pretended, it would have spread so extensively in one direction, and not at all in another? I make no exception in favour of the Carthagenians, whose origin was comparatively recent, and who, we know, were a colony from Asia."

I was obliged to admit the force of this reasoning; and, when he proceeded to descant on the former glories and achievements of Asiatic nations, and their sad reverses of fortune--while he freely spoke of the present degradation and imbecility of his countrymen, he promptly resisted every censure of mine. It was easy, indeed, to see that he secretly cherished a hope that the day would come, when the whole of Hindostan would be emancipated from its European masters, and assume that rank among nations to which the genius of its inhabitants entitled it. He admitted that the dominion of the English was less oppressive than that of their native princes; but said, that there was this great difference between foreign and domestic despotism,--that the former completely extinguished all national pride, which is as much the cause as the effect of national greatness.

I asked him whether he thought if his countrymen were to shake off the yoke of the English, they could maintain their independence?

"Undoubtedly," said he. "Who would be able to conquer us?"

I suggested to him that they might tempt the ambition of Russia; and cautiously inquired, whether the abstinence from animal food might not render his country much less capable of resistance; and whether it might not serve to explain why India had so often been the prey of foreign conquest? Of this, however, he would hear nothing; but replied, with more impatience than was usual with him--

"It is true, Hindostan was invaded by Alexander--but not conquered; and that it has since submitted, in succession, to the Arabians, to the Tartars, under Genghis Khan, and under Tamerlane; to the Persians, under Nadir Shah, and, finally, to the British. But there are few countries of Europe which have not been conquered as often. That nation from which you are descended, and to which mine is now subject, furnishes no exception, as it has been subjugated, in succession, by the Romans, the Danes, the Saxons, the Normans. And, as to courage, we see no difference between those Asiatics who eat animal food as you do, and those who abstain from it as I do. I am told that the Scotch peasantry eat much less animal food than the English, and the Irish far less than they; and yet, that these rank among the best troops of the British. But surely a nation ought not to be suspected of fearing death, whose very women show a contempt of life which no other people have exhibited."

This led us to talk of that strange custom of his country, which impels the widow to throw herself on the funeral pile of her husband, and to be consumed with him. I told him that it had often been represented as compulsory--or, in other words, that it was said that every art and means were resorted to, for the purpose of working on the mind of the woman, by her relatives, aided by the priests, who would be naturally gratified by such signal triumphs of religion over the strongest feelings of nature. He admitted that these engines were sometimes put in operation, and that they impelled to the sacrifice, some who were wavering; but insisted, that in a majority of instances the **Suttee** was voluntary.

"Women," said he, "are brought up from their infancy, to regard our sex as their superiors, and to believe that their greatest merit consists in entire devotion to their husbands. Under this feeling, and having, at the same time, their attention frequently turned to the chance of such a calamity, they are better prepared to meet it when it occurs. How few of the officers in your western armies, ever hesitate to march, at the head of their men, on a forlorn hope? and how many even court the danger for the sake of the glory? Nay, you tell me that, according to your code of honour, if one man insults another, he who gives the provocation, and he who receives it, rather than be disgraced in the eyes of their countrymen, will go out, and quietly shoot at each other with firearms, till one of them is killed or wounded; and this too, in many cases, when the injury has been merely nominal. If you show such a contempt of death, in deference to a custom founded in mere caprice, can it be wondered that a woman should show it, in the first paroxysms of her grief for the loss of him to whom was devoted every thought, word, and action of her life, and who, next to her God, was the object of her idolatry? My dear Atterley," he continued, with emotion, "you little know the strength of woman's love!"

Here he abruptly broke off the conversation; and, after continuing thoughtful and silent for some time, he remarked:

"But do not forget where we are. Nature demands her accustomed rest, and let us prepare to indulge her. I feel little inclined to sleep at present; yet, by the time you have taken some hours' repose, I shall probably require the same refreshment."

I would willingly have listened longer; but, yielding to his prudent suggestion, again composed myself to rest, and left my good monitor to his melancholy meditations. When I had slept about four hours, I was awakened by the Brahmin, in whose arms I found myself, and who, feeble as he was, handled me with the ease that a nurse does a child, or rather, as a child does her doll. On looking around, I found myself lying on what had been the ceiling of our chamber, which still, however, felt like the bottom. My eyes and my feelings were thus in collision, and I could only account for what I saw, by supposing that the machine had been turned upside down. I was bewildered and alarmed.

After enjoying my surprise for a moment, the Brahmin observed: "We have, while you were asleep, passed the middle point between the earth's and the moon's attraction, and we now gravitate less towards our own planet than her satellite. I took the precaution to move you, before you fell by your own gravity, from what was lately the bottom, to that which is now so, and to keep you in this place until you were retained in it by the moon's attraction; for, though your fall would have been, at this point, like that of a feather, yet it would have given you some shock and alarm. The machine, therefore, has undergone no change in its position or course; the change is altogether in our feelings."

The Brahmin then, after having looked through either telescope, but for a longer time through the one at the bottom, and having performed his customary devotions, soon fell into a slumber, but not into the same quiet sleep as before, for he was often interrupted by sudden starts, of so distressing a character, that I was almost tempted to wake him. After a while, however, he seemed more composed, when I betook myself to the telescope turned towards the earth.

The earth's appearance I found so diminished as not to exceed four times the diameter of the moon, as seen from the earth, and its whole face was entirely changed. After the first surprise, I recollected it was the moon I was then regarding, and my curiosity was greatly awakened. On raising myself up, and looking through the upper telescope, the earth presented an appearance not very dissimilar; but the outline of her continents and oceans were still perceptible, in different shades, and capable of being easily recognised; but the bright glare of the sun made the surfaces of both bodies rather dim and pale.

After a short interval, I again looked at the moon, and found not only its magnitude very greatly increased, but that it was beginning to present a more beautiful spectacle. The sun's rays fell obliquely on her disc, so that by a large part of its surface not reflecting the light, I saw every object on it, so far as I was enabled by the power of my telescope. Its mountains, lakes, seas, continents, and islands, were faintly, though not indistinctly, traced; and every moment brought forth something new to catch my eye, and awaken my curiosity. The whole face of the moon was of a silvery hue, relieved and varied by the softest and most delicate shades. No cloud nor speck of vapour intercepted my view. One of my exclamations of delight awakened the Brahmin, who quickly arose, and looking down on the resplendent orb below us, observed that we must soon begin to slacken the rapidity of our course, by throwing out ballast. The moon's dimensions now rapidly increased; the separate mountains, which formed the ridges and chains on her surface, began to be plainly visible through the telescope; whilst, on the shaded side, several volcanoes appeared upon her disc, like the flashes of our fire-fly, or rather like the twinkling of stars in a frosty night. He remarked, that the extraordinary clearness and brightness of the objects on the moon's surface, was owing to her having a less extensive and more transparent atmosphere than the earth: adding--"The difference is so great, that some of our astronomical observers have been induced to think she has none. If that, however, had been the case, our voyage would have been impracticable."

After gazing at the magnificent spectacle, with admiration and delight, for half an hour, the Brahmin loosed one of the balls of the lunar metal, for the purpose of checking our velocity. At this time he supposed we were not more than four thousand miles, or about twice the moon's diameter, from the nearest point of her surface. In about four hours more, her apparent magnitude was so great, that we could see her by looking out of either of the dark side-windows. Her disc had now lost its former silvery appearance, and began to look more like that of the earth, when seen at the same distance. It was a most gratifying spectacle to behold the objects successively rising to our view, and steadily enlarging in their dimensions. The rapidity with which we approached the moon, impressed me, in spite of myself, with the alarming sensation of falling; and I found myself alternately agitated with a sense of this danger, and with impatience to take a nearer view of the new objects that greeted my eyes. The Brahmin was wholly absorbed in calculations for the purpose of adjusting our velocity to the distance we had to go, his estimates of which, however, were in a great measure conjectural; and ever and anon he would let off a ball of the lunar metal.

After a few hours, we were so near the moon that every object was seen in our glass, as distinctly as the shells or marine plants through a piece of shallow sea-water, though the eye could take in but a small part of her surface, and the horizon, which bounded our view, was rapidly contracting. On letting the air escape from our machine, it did not now rush out with the same violence as before, which showed that we were within the moon's atmosphere. This, as well as ridding ourselves of the metal balls, aided in checking our progress. By and bye we were within a few miles of the highest mountains, when we threw down so much of our ballast, that we soon appeared almost stationary. The Brahmin remarked, that he should avail himself of the currents of air we might meet with, to select a favourable place for landing, though we were necessarily attracted towards the same region, in consequence of the same half of the moon's surface being always turned towards the earth.

"In our second voyage," said he, "we were glad to get foothold any where; for, not having lightened our machine sufficiently, we came down, with a considerable concussion, on a barren field, remote from any human habitation, and suffered more from hunger and cold, for nearly three days, than we had done from the perils and privations of the voyage. The next time we aimed at landing near the town of Alamatua, which stands, as you may see, a little to the right of us, upon an island in a lake, and looks like an emerald set in silver. We came down very gently, it is true, but we struck one of the numerous boats which ply around the island, and had nearly occasioned the loss of our lives, as well as of theirs. In our last voyage we were every way fortunate. The first part of the moon we approached, was a level plain, of great extent, divided into corn-fields, on which, having lowered our grapnel, we drew ourselves down without difficulty.

"We must now," continued he, "look out for some cultivated field, in one of the valleys we are approaching, where we may rely on being not far from some human abode, and on escaping the perils of rocks, trees, and buildings."

While the Brahmin was speaking, a gentle breeze arose, as appeared by our horizontal motion, which wafted us at the rate of about ten miles an hour, in succession, over a ridge of mountains, a lake, a thick wood, and a second lake, until at length we reached a cultivated region, recognised by the Brahmin as the country of the Morosofs, the place we were most anxious to reach.

"Let off two of the balls of lead to the earth," said he. I did so, and we descended rapidly. When we were sufficiently near the ground to see that it was a fit place for landing, we opened the door, and found the air of the moon inconceivably sweet and refreshing. We now loosed one of the lower balls, and somewhat checked our descent. In a few minutes more, however, we were within twenty yards of the ground, when we let go the largest ball of lunarium, which, having a cord attached to it, served us in lieu of a grapnel. It descended with great force to the ground, while the machine, thus lightened, was disposed to mount again. We, however, drew ourselves down; and as soon as the machine touched the ground, we let off some of our leaden balls to keep it there. We released ourselves from the machine in a twinkling; and our first impulse was to fall on our knees, and return thanks for our safe deliverance from the many perils of the voyage.

CHAPTER VI.

Some account of Morosofia, and its chief city Alamatua--Singular dresses of the Lunar ladies--Religious self denial--Glouglim miser and spendthrift.

My feelings, at the moment I touched the ground, repayed me for all I had endured. I looked around with the most intense curiosity; but nothing that I saw, surprised me so much as to find so little that was surprising. The vegetation, insects and other animals, were all pretty much of the same character as those I had seen before; but after I became better acquainted with them, I found the difference to be much greater than I at first supposed. Having refreshed ourselves with the remains of our stores, and secured the door of our machine, we bent our course, by a plain road, towards the town we saw on the side of a mountain, about three miles distant, and entered it a little before the sun had descended behind the adjacent mountain.

The town of Alamatua seemed to contain about two thousand houses, and to be not quite as large as Albany. The houses were built of a soft shining stone, and they all had porticoes, piazzas, and verandas, suited to the tropical climate of Morosofia. The people were tall and thin, of a pale yellowish complexion; and their garments light, loose, and flowing, and not very different from those of the Turks. The lower order of people commonly wore but a single garment, which passed round the waist. One half the houses were under ground, partly to screen them from the continued action of the sun's rays, and partly on account of the earthquakes caused by volcanoes. The windows of their houses were different from any I had ever seen before. They consisted of openings in the wall, sloping so much upwards, that while they freely admitted the light and air, the sun was completely excluded: and although those who were within could readily see what was passing in the streets, they were concealed from the gaze of the curious. In their hot-houses, it was common to have mirrors in the ceilings, which at once reflected the street passengers to those who were on the floor, and enabled the ostentatious to display to the public eye the decorations of their tables, whenever they gave a sumptuous feast.

The inhabitants subsist chiefly on a vegetable diet; live about as long as they do on the earth, notwithstanding the great difference of climate, and other circumstances; and, in short, do not, in their manners, habits, or character, differ more from the inhabitants of our planet, than some of these differ from one another. Their government was anciently monarchical, but is now popular. Their code of laws is said to be very intricate. Their language, naturally soft and musical, has been yet further refined by the cultivation of letters. They have a variety of sects in religion, politics, and philosophy. The territory of Morosofia is about 150 miles square. This brief sketch must content the reader for the present. I refer those who are desirous of being more particularly informed, to the work which I propose to publish on lunar geography; and, in the mean time, some of the most striking peculiarities of this people, in opinions, manners, and customs, will be developed in this, which must be considered as my ***personal narrative***.

As soon as we were espied by the inhabitants, we were surrounded by a troop of little boys, as well as all the idle and inquisitive near us. The Brahmin had not gone far, before he was met by some persons of his acquaintance, who immediately recognised him, and seemed very much pleased to see him again in the moon. They politely conducted us to the house of the governor, who received us very graciously. He appeared to be about forty-five years of age, was dressed in a pearl-coloured suit, and had a mild, amiable deportment. He began a course of interesting inquiry about the affairs of the earth; but a gentleman, whom we afterwards understood was one of the leaders of the popular party, coming in, he soon despatched us; having, however, first directed an officer to furnish us with all that was necessary for our accommodation, at the public expense--which act of hospitality, we have reason to fear, occasioned him some trouble and perplexity at the succeeding election. We very gladly withdrew, as both by reason of our long walk, and the excitement produced by so many new objects, we were greatly fatigued. The officer conducted us to respectable private lodgings, in a lightsome situation, which overlooked the chief part of the city.

After a frugal, but not unpalatable repast, and a few hours' sleep, the Brahmin took me round the city and a part of its environs, to make me acquainted with the public buildings, streets, shops, and the appearance of the inhabitants. I soon found that our arrival was generally known and that we excited quite as much curiosity as we felt, though many of the persons we met had seen the Brahmin before. I was surprised that we saw none of their women; but the Brahmin told me that they were every where gazing through their windows; and, on looking up, through these slanting apertures I could often see their eyes peeping over the upper edge of the window-sill.

I shall now proceed to record faithfully what I deem most memorable; not as many travellers have done, from their recollection, after their return home, but from notes, which I regularly made, either at the moment of observation, or very shortly afterwards. When we first visited the shops, I was equally gratified and surprised with what was familiar and what was new; but I was particularly amused with those of the tailors and milliners. In the lower part of their dress, the Lunarians chiefly resemble the Europeans; but in the upper part, the Asiatics--for they shave the head, and wear turbans; from which fact the Brahmin drew another argument in favour of the hypothesis, that the moon was originally a part of the earth. Some of the female fashions were so extremely singular and fanciful, as to deserve particular mention.

One piece of their attire was formed of a long piece of light stiff wood, covered with silk, and decorated with showy ornaments. It was worn across the shoulders, beyond each of which it jutted out about half a yard; and from either end a cord led to a ring running round the upper part of the head, bearing no small resemblance to the yard of a ship's mast, and the ropes used for steering it. Several other dresses I saw, which I am satisfied would be highly disapproved by my modest countrywomen. Thus, in some were inserted glasses like watch crystals, adapted to the form and size of the female bosom. But, to do the Lunar ladies justice, I understood that these dresses were condemned by the sedate part of the sex, and were worn only by the young and thoughtless, who were vain of their forms. I observed too, that instead of decorating their heads with flowers, like the ladies of our earth, they taxed the animal world for a correspondent ornament. Many of the head-dresses were made of a stiff open gauze, occasionally stuck over with insects of the butterfly and *coccinella* species, and others of the gayest hues. At other times these insects were alive; when their perpetual buzzing and fluttering in their transparent cages, had a very animating effect. One decoration for the head in particular struck my fancy: it was formed of a silver tissue, containing fireflies, and intended to be worn in the night.

But the most remarkable thing of all, was the whim of the ladies in the upper classes, of making themselves as much like birds as possible; in which art, it must be confessed, they were wonderfully successful. The dress used for this purpose, consisted of a sort of thick cloak, covered with feathers, like those of the South Sea islands, and was so fashioned, by means of a tight thick quilting, as to make the wearer, at a little distance, very much resemble an overgrown bird, except that the legs were somewhat too thick. Their arms were concealed under the wings; and the resemblance was yet further increased, by marks with beaks adapted to the particular plumage: some personating doves, some magpies; others again, hawks, parrots, &c., according to their natural figure, humour, &c.; while the deception was still further assisted by their extraordinary agility, compared with ours, by means of which they could, with ease, hop eighteen or twenty feet. I told the Brahmin that some of the Indians of our continent showed a similar taste in dress, by decorating themselves with horns like the buffalo, and with tails like horses; which furnished him with a further argument in favour of a common origin.

We spent above an hour in examining these curious habiliments, and in inquiring the purposes and uses of the several parts. Sometimes I was induced, through the Brahmin, to criticise their taste and skill, having been always an admirer of simplicity in female attire. But I remarked on this occasion, as on several others, subsequently, that the people of the moon were neither very thankful for advice, nor thought very highly of the judgment of those who differ from them in opinion.

After having rambled over the city about six hours, our appetites told us it was time to return to our lodgings; and here I met with a new cause of wonder. The family with whom we were domesticated, belonged to a numerous and zealous sect of religionists, and were, in their way, very worthy, as well as pious people. Their dinner consisted of several dishes of vegetables, variously served up; of roots, stalks, seeds, flowers, and fruits, some of which resembled the productions of the earth; and in particular, I saw a dish of what I at first took to be very fine asparagus, but supposed I was mistaken, when I saw them eat the coarse fibrous part alone. On tasting it, however, in the ordinary way, I found it to be genuine, good asparagus; but I perceived that the family looked extremely shocked at my taste. After the other dishes were removed, some large fruit, of the peach kind, were set on the table, when the members of the family, having carefully paired off the skin, ate it, and threw the rest away. They in like manner chewed the shells of some small grayish nuts, and threw away the kernels, which to me were very palatable. The younger children, consisting of two boys and a girl, exchanged looks with each other at the selections I made, and I thought I perceived in the looks of the mother, still more aversion than surprise. I found too, that my friend the Brahmin abstained from all these things, and partook only of those vegetables and fruits of which both they and I ate alike. Some wine was offered us, which appeared to me to be neither more nor less than vinegar; and, what added to my surprise, a bottle, which they said was not yet fit to drink, seemed to me to be pretty good, the Brahmin having passed it to me for my judgment, as soon as they pronounced upon it sentence of condemnation.

After we arose from this strange scene, and had withdrawn to our chamber, I expressed my surprise to my companion at this contrariety in the tastes of the Terrestrials and Lunarians: whereupon he told me, that the difference was rather apparent than real.

"These people," said he, "belong to a sect of Ascetics in this country, who are persuaded that all pleasure received through the senses is sinful, and that man never appears so acceptable in the sight of the Deity, as when he rejects all the delicacies of the palate, as well as other sensual gratifications, and imposes on himself that food to which he feels naturally most repugnant. You may see that those peaches, which were so disdainfully thrown into the yard, are often secretly picked up by the children, who obey the impulses of nature, and devour them most greedily. Even in the old people themselves, there is occasionally some backsliding into the depravity of worldly appetite. You might have perceived, that while the old man was abusing the wine you drank as unripe, and making wry faces at it, he still kept tasting it; and if I had not reached it to you, he would probably, before he had ceased his meditations, have finished half the bottle. It must be confessed, that although religion cherishes our best feelings, it also often proves a cloak for the worst."

I told him that our clergy were superior to this weakness, most of them manifesting a proper sense of the bounty of Providence, by eating and drinking of the best, (not very sparingly neither); and that in New-York, we considered some of our preachers the best judges of wine among us. Soon afterwards, we again sallied forth in quest of adventures, and bent our course towards the suburbs.

We had not gone far, before we saw several persons looking at a man working hard at a forge, in a low crazy building. On approaching him, we found he was engaged in making nails, an operation which he performed with great skill and adroitness; and as soon as he had made as many as he could take up in his hand at once, he carried them behind his little hovel, and dropped them into a narrow deep well. Some of the by-standers wished to beg a few of what he seemed to value so lightly, and others offered to give him bread or clothes in exchange for his nails, but he obstinately resisted all their applications; in fact, little heeding them, although he was almost naked, had a starved, haggard appearance, and evidently regarded the food they proffered with a wishful eye.

The lookers on told us the blacksmith had been for years engaged in this business of nail-making; he worked with little intermission, scarcely allowing himself time for necessary sleep or refreshment; that all the fruits of his incessant labour were disposed of in the manner we had just seen; and that he had already three wells filled with nails, which he had carefully closed. He had, moreover, a large and productive farm, the increase arising from which, was laid out in exchange for the metal of which his nails were made. He had, we were informed, so much attachment to these pieces of metal, that he was often on the point of starvation before he would part with one.

I observed to the Brahmin, that it was a singular, and somewhat inexplicable, species of madness.

"True," he replied; "this man's conduct cannot be explained upon any rational principles--but he is one of the Glonglims, of which I have spoken to you; and examples are not wanting on our planet, of conduct as irreconcilable to reason. This man is making an article which is scarce, as well as useful, in this country, where gravity is less than it is with us: the force of the wind is very great, and the metal is possessed but by a few. Now, if you suppose these nails to be pieces of gold and silver, his conduct will be precisely that of some of our misers, who waste their days and nights in hoarding up wealth which they never use, nor mean to use; but, denying themselves every comfort of life, anxiously and unceasingly toil for those who are to come after them, though they are so far from feeling, towards these successors, any peculiar affection, that they often regard them with jealousy and hatred."

While we thus conversed, there stepped up to us a handsome man, foppishly dressed in blue trowsers, a pink vest, and a red and white turban; who, after having shaken my companion by the ears, according to the custom of the country among intimate friends, expressed his delight at seeing him again in Morosofia. He then went on, in a lively, humorous strain, to ridicule the nail-smith, and told us several stories of his singular attachment to his nails. In the midst of these sallies, however, a harsh looking personage in brown came up, upon which the countenance of our lively acquaintance suddenly changed, and they walked off together.

"I apprehend," said the Brahmin, "that my gay acquaintance yonder continues as he formerly was. The man in brown, who so unseasonably interrupted his pleasantry, is an officer of justice, and has probably taken him before a magistrate, to answer some one of his numerous creditors. You must know," added he, "that the people of the moon, however irrational themselves, are very prompt in perceiving the absurdities of others: and this lively wit, who, as you see, wants neither parts nor address, acts as strangely as the wretch he has been ridiculing. He inherited a large estate, which brought him in a princely revenue; and yet his desires and expenses so far outgo his means, that he is always in want. Both he and the nailmaker suffer the evils of poverty-- of poverty created by themselves--which, moreover, they can terminate when they please; but they must reach the same point by directly opposite roads. The blacksmith will allow himself nothing--the beau will deny himself nothing: the one is a slave to pleasure--the other, the victim of fear. I told you that there were but few whose estates produced the metal of which these nails are made; and this thoughtless youth happens to be one. A few years since, he wanted some of the blacksmith's nails to purchase the first rose of the season, and pledged his mines to pay, at the end of the year, three times the amount he received in exchange; and although, if he were to use but half his income for a single year, the other half would discharge his debts. I apprehend, from what I have heard, that he has, from that time to this, continued to pay the same exorbitant interest. When I was here before, I prevailed on him to take a ride with me into the country, and, under one pretext or another, detained him ten days at a friend's house, where he had no inducement to expense. When he returned, he found his debts paid off; but knowing he was master of so ready and effectual an expedient, he, the next day, borrowed double the sum at the old rate. Since that time his debts have accumulated so rapidly, that he will probably now be compelled to surrender his whole estate."

"Is he also a Glonglim?" I asked.

"Assuredly: what man, in his entire senses, could act so irrationally?"

"There is nothing on earth that exceeds this," said I.

"No," said the Brahmin; "human folly is every where the same."

CHAPTER VII.

Physical peculiarities of the Moon-Celestial phenomena--Further description of the Lunarians--National prejudice--Lightness of bodies--The Brahmin carries Atterley to sup with a philosopher--His character and opinions.

After we had been in the moon about forty eight hours, the sun had sunk below the horizon, and the long twilight of the Lunarians had begun. I will here take occasion to notice the physical peculiarities of this country, which, though very familiar to those who are versed in astronomy, may not be unacceptable to the less scientific portion of my readers.

The sun is above the horizon nearly a fortnight, and below it as long; of course the day here is equal to about twenty-seven of ours. The earth answers the same purpose to half the inhabitants of the moon, that the moon does to the inhabitants of the earth. The face of the latter, however, is more than twelve times as large, and it has not the same silvery appearance as the moon, but is rather of a dingy pink hue, like that of her iron when beginning to lose its red heat. As the same part of the moon is always turned to the earth, one half of her surface is perpetually illuminated by a moon ten times as large to the eye as the sun; the other hemisphere is without a moon. The favoured part, therefore, never experiences total darkness, the earth reflecting to the Lunarians as much light as we terrestrials have a little before sunrise, or after sunset. But our planet presents to the Lunarians the same changes as the moon does to us, according to its position in relation to the sun. It always, however, appears to occupy nearly the same part of the heavens, when seen from the same point on the moon's surface; but its altitude above the horizon is greater or less, according to the latitude of the place from which it is seen: so that there is not a point of the heavens which the earth may not be seen permanently to occupy, according to the part of the moon from which the planet is viewed.

From the length of time that the sun is above the horizon, the continued action of his rays, in those climates where they fall vertically, or nearly so, would be intolerable, if it was not for the high mountains, from whose snow-clad summits a perpetual breeze derives a refreshing coolness, and for the deep glens and recesses, in which most animals seek protection from his meridian beams. The transitions from heat to cold are less than one would expect, from the length of their days and nights--the coolness of the one, as well as the heat of the other, being tempered by a constant east wind. The climate gradually becomes colder as we approach the Poles; but there is little or no change of seasons in the same latitude.

The inhabitants of the moon have not the same regularity in their meals, or time for sleep, as we have, but consult their appetites and inclinations like other animals. But they make amends for this irregularity, by a very strict and punctilious observance of festivals, which are regulated by the motions of the sun, at whose rising and setting they have their appropriate ceremonies. Those which are kept at sunrise, are gay and cheerful, like the hopes which the approach of that benignant luminary inspires. The others are of a grave and sober character, as if to prepare the mind for serious contemplation in their long-enduring night. When the earth is at the full, which is their midnight, it is also a season of great festivity with them.

Eclipses of the sun are as common with the Lunarians as those of the moon are with us--the same relative position of the three bodies producing this phenomenon; but an *eclipse of the earth* never takes place, as the shadow of the moon passes over the broad disc of our planet, merely as a dark spot.

The inhabitants of the moon can always determine both their latitude and longitude, by observing the quarter of the heavens in which the earth is seen: and, as the sun invariably appears of the same altitude at their noon, the inhabitants are denominated and classed according to the length of their shadows; and the terms *long shadow*, or *short shadow*, are common forms of national reproach among them, according to the relative position of the parties. I found the climate of those whose shadows are about the length of their own figure, the most agreeably to my own feelings, and most like that of my own country.

Such are the most striking natural appearances on one side of this satellite.

On the other there is some difference. The sun pursues the same path in the corresponding latitudes of both hemispheres; but being without any moon, they have a dull and dreary night, though the light from the stars is much greater than with us. The science of astronomy is much cultivated by the inhabitants of the dark hemisphere, and is indebted to them for its most important discoveries, and its present high state of improvement.

If there is much rivalship among the natives of the same hemisphere, who differ in the length of their shadows, they all unite in hatred and contempt for the inhabitants of the opposite side. Those who have the benefit of a moon, that is, who are turned towards the earth, are lively, indolent, and changeable as the face of the luminary on which they pride themselves; while those on the other side are more grave, sedate, and industrious. The first are called the Hilliboos, and the last the Moriboos--or bright nights, and dark nights. And this mutual animosity is the more remarkable, as they often appeared to me to be the same race, and to differ much less from one another than the natives of different climates. It is true, that enlightened and well educated men do not seem to feel this prejudice, or at least they do not show it: but those who travel from one hemisphere to the other, are sure to encounter the prejudices of the vulgar, and are often treated with great contempt and indignity. They are pointed at by the children, who, according as they chance to have been bred on one side or the other say, "There goes a man who never saw Glootin," as they call the earth; or, "There goes a Booblimak," which means a night stroller.

All bodies are much lighter on the moon than on the earth; by reason of which circumstance, as has been mentioned, the inhabitants are more active, and experience much less fatigue in ascending their precipitous mountains. I was astonished at first at this seeming increase in my muscular powers; when, on passing along a street in Alamatua, soon after my arrival, and meeting a dog, which I thought to be mad, I proposed to run out of his way, and in leaping over a gutter, I fairly bounded across the street. I measured the distance the next day, and found it to be twenty-seven feet five inches; and afterwards frequently saw the school-boys, when engaged in athletic exercises, make running leaps of between thirty and forty feet, backwards and forwards. Another consequence of the diminished gravity here is, that both men and animals carry much greater burdens than on the earth.

The carriages are drawn altogether by dogs, which are the largest animals they have, except the zebra, and a small buffalo. This diminution of gravity is, however, of some disadvantage to them. Many of their tools are not as efficient as ours, especially their axes, hoes, and hammers. On the other hand, when a person falls to the ground, it is nearly the same thing as if an inhabitant of the earth were to fall on a feather bed. Yet I saw as many instances of fractured limbs, hernia, and other accidents there, as I ever saw on the earth; for when they fall from great heights, or miscarry in the feats of activity which they ambitiously attempt, it inflicts the same injury upon them, as a fall nearer the ground does upon us.

After we had been here sufficiently long to see what was most remarkable in the city, and I had committed the fruit of my observations to paper, the Brahmin proposed to carry me to one of the monthly suppers of a philosopher whom he knew, and who had obtained great celebrity by his writings and opinions.

We accordingly went, and found him sitting at a small table, and apparently exhausted with the labour of composition, and the ardour of intense thought. He was a small man, of quick, abrupt manners, occasionally very abstracted, but more frequently voluble, earnest, and disputatious. He frankly told us he was sorry to see us, as he was then putting the last finish to a great and useful work he was about to publish: that we had thus unseasonably broken the current of his thoughts, and he might not be able to revive it for some days. Upon my rising to take my leave, he assured me that it would be adding to the injury already done, if we then quitted him. He said he wished to learn the particulars of our voyage; and that he, in turn, should certainly render us service, by disclosing some of the results of his own reflections. He further remarked, that he expected six or eight friends--that is, (correcting himself,) "enlightened and congenial minds," to supper, on the rising of a constellation he named, which time, he remarked, would soon arrive. Finding his frankness to be thus seasoned with hospitality, we resumed our seats. It soon appeared that he was more disposed to communicate information than to seek it; and I became a patient listener. If the boldness and strangeness of his opinions occasionally startled me, I could not but admire the clearness with which he stated his propositions, the fervour of his elocution, and the plausibility of his arguments.

The expected guests at length arrived; and various questions of morals and legislation were started, in which the disputants seemed sometimes as if they would have laid aside the character of philosophers, but for the seasonable interposition of the Brahmin. Wigurd, our host, often laboured with his accustomed zeal, to prove that every one who opposed him, was either a fool, or biassed by some petty interest, or the dupe of blind prejudice.

After about two hours of warm, and, as it seemed to me, unprofitable discussion, we were summoned to our repast in the adjoining room. But before we rose from our seats, our host requested to know of each of us if we were hungry; and, whether it were from modesty, perverseness, or really because they had no appetite, I know not, but a majority of the company, in which I was included, voted that their hour of eating was not yet come: upon which Wigurd remarked that his own vote, as being at home, and the Brahmin's, as being at once a philosopher and a stranger, should each count for two; and by this mode of reckoning there was a casting vote in favour of going to supper.

We found the table covered with tempting dishes, served up in a costly and tasteful style, and a sprightly, well-looking female prepared to do the honours of the feast. She reproved our host for his delay, and told him the best dish was spoiled, by being cold. I was fearful of a discussion; but he sat down without making a reply, and immediately addressing the company, descanted on the various qualities of food, and their several adaptations to different ages, constitutions, and temperaments. He condemned the absurd practice which prevailed, for the master or mistress of the house to lavish entreaties on their guests to eat that which they might be better without; and insisted, at the same time, that the guests ought not to consult their own tastes exclusively. He maintained, that the only course worthy of rational and benevolent beings, was for every man to judge for his neighbour as well as for himself; and, should any collision arise between the different claimants, then, if any one were guided by that decision, which an honest and unbiassed judgment would tell him was right, they would all come to the same just and harmonious result.

"But," added he, "you have not yet been sufficiently prepared for this disinterested operation. As ye have proved this night that ye are not yet purged of the feelings and prejudices of a vicious education, I will perform this office for you all, and set you an example, by which ye may hereafter profit. To begin, then, with you-- (addressing himself to a corpulent man, of a florid complexion, at the lower end of the table:)--As you already have a redundancy of flesh and blood, I assign the *soupe maigre* to you; while to our mathematical friend on this side, whose delicate constitution requires nourishment, I recommend the smoking ragout. This cooling dish will suit your temperament," said he to a third; "and this stimulating one, yours," to a fourth. "Those little birds, which cost me five pieces, I shall divide between my terrestrial friend here (looking at the Brahmin) and myself, we being the most meritorious of the company, and it being of the utmost importance to society, that food so wholesome should give nourishment to our bodies, and impart vigour and vivacity to our minds."

From this decision there was no appeal, and no other dissent than what was expressed by a look or a low murmur. But I perceived the corpulent gentleman and the wan mathematician slily exchange their dishes, by which they both seemed to consider themselves gainers. The dish allotted to me, being of a middling character, I ate of it without repining; though, from the savoury fumes of my right-hand neighbour's plate, I could not help wishing I had been allowed to choose for myself.

This supper happening near the middle of the night, (at which time it was always pretty cool,) a cheerful fire blazed in one side of the room and I perceived that our host and hostess placed themselves so as to be at the most agreeable distance, the greater part of the guests being either too near or too far from it.

After we had finished our repast, various subjects of speculation were again introduced and discussed, greatly to my amusement. Wigurd displayed his usual ingenuity and ardour, and baffled all his antagonists by his vehemence and fluency. He had two great principles by which he tested the good or evil of every thing; and there were few questions in which he could not avail himself of one or the other. These were, general *utility* and *truth*.

By a skilful use of these weapons of controversy, he could attack or defend with equal success. If any custom or institution which he had denounced, was justified by his adversaries, on the ground of its expediency, he immediately retorted on them its repugnancy to sincerity, truth, and unsophisticated nature; and if they, at any time, resorted to a similar justification for our natural feelings and propensities, he triumphantly showed that they were inimical to the public good. Thus, he condemned gratitude as a sentiment calculated to weaken the sense of justice, and to substitute feeling for reason. He, on the other hand, proscribed the little forms and courtesies, which are either founded in convenience, or give a grace and sweetness to social intercourse, as a direct violation of honest nature, and therefore odious and mean. He thus was able to silence every opponent. I was very desirous of hearing the Brahmin's opinion; but, while he evidently was not convinced by our host's language, he declined engaging in any controversy.

After we retired, my friend told me that Wigurd was a good man in the main, though he had been as much hated by some as if his conduct had been immoral, instead of his opinions merely being singular. "He not long ago," added the Brahmin "wrote a book against marriage, and soon afterwards wedded, in due form, the lady you saw at his table. She holds as strange tenets as he, which she supports with as much zeal, and almost as much ability. But I predict that the popularity of their doctrines will not last; and if ever you visit the moon again, you will find that their glory, now at its height, like the ephemeral fashions of the earth, will have passed away."

CHAPTER VIII.

A celebrated physician: his ingenious theories in physics: his mechanical inventions--The feather-hunting Glonglim.

On returning to our lodgings, we, acting under the influence of long habit, went to bed, though half the family were up, and engaged in their ordinary employments. One consequence of the length of the days and nights here is, that every household is commonly divided into two parts, which watch and sleep by turns: nor have they any uniformity in their meals, except in particular families, which are regulated by clocks and time-pieces. The vulgar have no means of measuring smaller portions of time than a day or night, (each equal to a fortnight with us,) except by observing the apparent motion of the sun or the stars, in which, considering that it is nearly thirty times as slow as with us, they attain surprising accuracy. They have the same short intervals of labour and rest in their long night as their day--the light reflected from the earth, being commonly sufficient to enable them to perform almost any operation; and, ere our planet is in her second quarter, one may read the smallest print by her light.

To compensate their want of this natural advantage, the inhabitants of Moriboozia are abundantly supplied with a petroleum, or bituminous liquid, which is found every where about their lakes, or on their mountains, and which they burn in lamps, of various sizes, shapes, and constructions. They have also numerous volcanoes, each of which sheds a strong light for many miles around.

We slept unusually long; and, owing in part to Wigurd's good cheer, I awoke with a head-ache. I got up to take a long walk, which often relieves me when suffering from that malady; and, on ascending the stairs, I met our landlord's eldest daughter, a tall, graceful girl of twenty. I found she was coming down backwards, which I took to be a mere girlish freak, or perhaps a piece of coquetry, practised on myself: but I afterwards found, that about the time the earth is at the full, the whole family pursued the same course, and were very scrupulous in making their steps in this awkward and inconvenient way, because it was one of the prescribed forms of their church.

As my head-ache became rather worse, than better, from my walk, the Brahmin proposed to accompany me to the house of a celebrated physician, called Vindar, who was also a botanist, chemist, and dentist, to consult him on my case; and thither we forthwith proceeded. I found him a large, unwieldy figure, of a dull, heavy look, but by no means deficient in science or natural shrewdness. He confirmed my previous impression that I ought to lose blood, and plausibly enough accounted for my present sensation of fulness, from the inferior pressure of the lunar atmosphere to that which I had been accustomed. He proposed, however, to return to my veins a portion of thinner blood in place of what he should take away, and offered me the choice of several animals, which he always kept by him for that purpose. There were two white animals of the hog kind, a male and a female lama, three goats, besides several birds, about the size of a turkey, some tortoises, and other amphibious animals. He professed himself willing, in case I had any foolish scruples against mixing my blood with that of brutes, to purify my own, and put it back; but I obstinately declined both expedients; whereupon he opened a vein in my arm, and took from it about fourteen ounces of blood. Finding myself, weakened as well as relieved, by the operation, he invited me to rest myself; and while I was recovering my strength, he discoursed with the Brahmin and myself on several of his favourite topics. On returning home, I committed to paper some of the most remarkable of his opinions, which it may be as well to notice, that those who have since propounded, or may hereafter propound, the same to the world, may not claim the merit of originality.

He maintained that the number of our senses was greater than that commonly assigned to us. That we had, for example, a sense of acids, of alkalies, of weight, and of heat. That acid substances acted upon our bodies by a peculiar set of nerves, or through some medium of their own, was evident from this, that they set the teeth on edge, though these, from their hard and bony nature, are insensible to the touch. That astringents shrivelled up the flesh and puckered the mouth, even when their taste was not perceived. That when the skin shrunk on the application of vinegar, could it be said that it had not a peculiar sense of this liquid, or rather of its acidity, since the existence of the senses was known only by effects which external matter produced on them? That the senses, like that of touch, were seated in most parts of the body, but were most acute in the mouth, nose, ears, and eyes. He showed some disposition to maintain the popular notions of the Greeks and Romans, that the rivers and streams are endowed with reason and volition; and endeavoured to prove that some of their windings and deviations from a straight line, cannot be explained upon mechanical principles.

Vindar is, moreover, a projector of a very bold character; and not long ago petitioned the commanding general of an army, suddenly raised to repel an incursion of one of their neighbours, to march his troops into Goolo-Tongtoia, for the purpose of digging a canal from one of their petroleum lakes into Morosofia, and conducting it, by smaller streams, over that country, for the purpose of warming it during their long cool nights.

He has, too, a large grist and saw mill, which are put in motion by the explosion of gunpowder. This is conveyed, by a sufficiently ingenious machine, in very small portions, to the bottom of an upright cylinder, which is immediately shut perfectly close. A flint and steel are at the same time made to strike directly over it, and to ignite the powder. The air that is thus generated, forces up a piston through a cylinder, which piston, striking the arm of a wheel, puts it in motion, and with it the machinery of the mills. A complete revolution of the wheel again prepares the cylinder for a fresh supply of gunpowder, which is set on fire, and produces the same effect as before.

He told me he had been fifteen years perfecting this great work, in which time it had been twice blown up by accidents, arising from the carelessness or mismanagement of the workmen; but that he now expected it would repay him for the time and money he had expended. He had once, he said, intended to use the expansive force of congelation for his moving power; but he found, after making a full and accurate calculation, that the labourers required to keep the machine supplied with ice, consumed something more than twice as much corn as the mill would grind in the same time. He then was about to move it to a fine stream of water in the neighbourhood, which, by being dammed up, so as to form a large pond, would afford him a convenient and inexhaustible supply of ice. But the millwright, after the dam was completed, having artfully obtained his permission to use the waste water, and fraudulently erected there a common water-mill, which soon obtained all the neighbouring custom, he had sold out that property, and resorted to the agency of gunpowder, which is quite as philosophical a process as that of congelation, and much less expensive. In answer to an inquiry of the Brahmin's, he admitted, that though he had been able, by the force of congelation, to burst metallic tubes several inches thick, he had never succeeded in making it put the lightest machinery into a continued motion.

Having now nearly recovered, and being, I confess, somewhat bewildered by the variety and complexity of these ingenious projects, I felt disposed to take my leave; but Vindar insisted on conducting us into an inner apartment, to see his ***poetry box***. This was a large piece of furniture, profusely decorated with metals of various colours, curiously and fantastically inlaid. It contained a prodigious number of drawers, which were labelled after the manner of those in an apothecary's shop, (from whence he denied, however, that he first took the hint,) and the labels were arranged in alphabetical order.

"Now," says he, "as the excellence of poetry consists in bringing before the mind's eye what can be brought before the corporeal eye, I have here collected every object that is either beautiful or pleasing in nature, whether by its form, colour, fragrance, sweetness, or other quality, as well as those that are strikingly disagreeable. When I wish to exhibit those pictures which constitute poetry, I consult the appropriate cabinet, and I take my choice of those various substances which can best call up the image I wish to present to my reader. For example: suppose I wish to speak of any object that is white, or analogous to white, I open the drawer that is thus labelled, and I see silver, lime, chalk, and white enamel, ivory, paper, snow-drops, and alabaster, and select whichever of these substances will best suit the measure and the rhyme, and has the most soft-sounding name. If the colour be yellow, then there are substances of all shades of this hue, from saffron and pickled salmon to brimstone and straw. I have sixty-two red substances, twenty-seven green ones, and others in the same proportion. It is astonishing what labour this box has saved me, and how much it has added to the beauty and melody of my verse.

"You perceive," he added, "the drawer missing. That contained substances offensive to the sight or smell, which my maid, conducted to it by her nose, conceived to be some animal curiosities I had been collecting, in a state of putrefaction and decay, and did not hesitate to throw them into the fire. I afterwards found myself very much at a loss, whenever my subject led me to the mention of objects of this character, and I therefore spoke of them as seldom as possible." After bestowing that tribute of admiration and praise which every great author or inventor expects, in his own house, and not omitting his customary medical fee, we took our leave.

We had not long left Vindar's house, before we saw a short fat man in the suburbs, preparing to climb to the top of a plane tree, on which there was one of the tail feathers of a sort of flamingo. He was surrounded by attendants and servants, to whom he issued his commands with great rapidity and decision, occasionally intermingling with his orders the most threatening language and furious gesticulations. Some offered to get a ladder, and ascend, and others to cut down the tree; all of which he obstinately rejected. He swore he would get the feather--he would get it by climbing--and he would climb but one way, which way was on the shoulders of his men. His plan was to make a number of them form a solid square, and interlock their arms; then a smaller number to mount upon their shoulders, on whom others were in like manner placed, and so on till the pyramid was sufficiently high, when he himself was to mount, and from the shoulders of the highest pluck the darling object of his wishes. He had in this way, I afterwards learnt, gathered some of the richest flowers of the bignonia scarlatina, as well as such fruits as had tempted him by their luscious appearance, and at the same time frightening all the birds from their nests, which he commonly destroyed: and although some of his attendants were occasionally much hurt and bruised in this singular amusement, he still persevered in it. He had continued it for several years, with no intermission, except a short one, when he was engaged in breaking a young llana in the place of an old one, which had been many years a favourite, but was now in disgrace, because, as he said, he did not think it so safe for going down hill, but in reality, because he liked the figure and movements of the young one better.

I could not see this rash Glonglim attempt to climb that dangerous ladder, without feeling alarm for his safety. At first all seemed to go on very well; but just as he was about to lay hold of the gaudy prize, there arose a sudden squall, which threw both him and his supporters into confusion, and the whole living pyramid came to the ground together. Many were killed--some were wounded and bruised. Polenap himself, by lighting on his men, who served him as cushions, barely escaped with life. But he received a fracture in the upper part of his head, and a dislocation of the hip, which will not only prevent him from ever climbing again, but probably make him a cripple for life.

The Brahmin and I endeavoured to give the sufferers some assistance; but this was rendered unnecessary, by the crowd which their cries and lamentations brought to their relief. I thought that the author of so much mischief would have been stoned on the spot; but, to my surprise, his servants seemed to feel as much for his honour as their own safety, and warmly interfered in his behalf, until they had somewhat appeased the rage of the surrounding multitude.

CHAPTER IX.

The fortune-telling philosopher, who inspected the finger nails: his visiters--Another philosopher, who judged of the character by the hair--The fortune-teller duped--Predatory warfare.

As we returned to our lodgings, we saw a number of persons, some of whom were entering and some leaving a neat small dwelling; and on joining the throng, we learnt that a famous fortune-teller lived there, who, at stated periods, opened his house to all that were willing to pay for being instructed in the events of futurity, or for having the secrets of the present or past revealed to them. On entering the house, and descending a flight of steps, we found, at the farther end of a dark room, lighted with a chandelier suspended from the ceiling, an elderly man, with a long gray beard, and a thin, pale countenance, deeply furrowed with thought rather than care. He received us politely, and then resumed the duties of his vocation. His course of proceeding was to examine the finger nails, and, according to their form, colour, thickness, surface, and grain, to determine the character and destinies of those who consulted him. I was at once pleased and surprised at the minuteness of his observation, and the infinite variety of his distinctions. Besides the qualities of the nails that I have mentioned, he noticed some which altogether eluded my senses, such as their milkiness, flintiness, friability, elasticity, tenacity, and sensibility; whether they were aqueous, unctious, or mealy; with many more, which have escaped my recollection.

A modest, pensive looking girl, apparently about seventeen, was timidly holding forth her hand for examination, at the time we entered. Avarabet, (for that was the name of this philosopher,) uttered two or three words, with a significant shake of his head, upon which I saw the rising tear in her eyes. She withdrew her hand,

and had not courage to let him take another look.

A fat woman, of a sanguine temperament, holding a little girl by the hand, then stepped up and showed her fingers. He pronounced her amorous, inconstant, prone to anger, and extravagant; that she had made one man miserable, and would probably make another. She also abruptly withdrew, giving manifest signs of one of the qualities ascribed to her.

An elderly matron then approached, holding forth one trembling, palsied hand, with a small volume in the other. Avarabet hesitated for some time; examined the edges as well as the surface of the nails; drew his finger slowly over them, and then said,--"You have a susceptible heart; you are in sorrow, but your affliction will soon have an end." It was easy to see, in the look of the applicant, signs of pious resignation, and a lively hope of another and a better state of existence.

I thought I perceived in the scene that was passing before us, an exhibition that is not uncommon on our earth, of cunning knavery imposing on ignorance and credulity; and I expressed my opinion to the Brahmin; but he assured me that the class of persons in the moon, who were resorted to on account of their supposed powers of divination, was very different from the similar class in Asia or Europe, and that oracular art was here regularly studied and professed as a branch of philosophy. "You would be surprised," said he, "to find how successful they have been in investing their craft with the forms and trappings of science, the parade of classification, and the mystery imparted by technical terms. By these means they have given plausibility enough to their theories, to leave many a one in doubt, whether it is really a new triumph of human discovery, or merely a later form of empiricism. Its professors are commonly converts to their own theories, at least in a great degree; for, strange as it may seem, there can mingle with the disposition to deceive others, the power of deceiving one's self; and while they exercise much acuteness and penetration in discovering, by the air, look, dress, and manner of those who consult them, the leading points in the history or character of persons of whom they have no previous knowledge, they at the same time persuade themselves that they see something indicative of their circumstances in their finger nails. Such is the equivocal character of the greater part of their sect: but there are some who are mere honest dupes to the pretensions of the science; and others again, who have not one tittle of credulity to extenuate their impudent pretensions.

"When I was here before, I remember a physician, who acquired great celebrity by affecting to cure diseases by examining a lock of the patient's hair; and, not content with merely pronouncing on the nature of the disease, and suggesting the remedy, he would enter into an elaborate, and often plausible course of reasoning, in defence of his system. That system was briefly this: that the hair derived its length, strength, hue, and other properties, from the brain; which opinion he supported by a reference to acknowledged facts--as, that it changes its hue with the difference of the mental character in the different stages of life; that violent affections of the mind, such as grief or fear, have been known to change it in a single night. Science on this, as on other occasions, is merely augmenting and methodizing facts that the mass of mankind had long observed--as, that red hair had always been considered indicative of warm temperament; that affliction, and even love, were believed to create baldness; and that in great terror, the hair stands on end. The different ages too, are distinguished as much by their hair as their complexion, their facial angle, or in any other way. He was led to this theory first, by observing at school that a boy of a stiff, bristly head of hair, was remarkably cruel. He professed to have been able, from a long course of observation, to assign to every different colour and variety of hair, its peculiar temperament and character. One mental quality was indicated by its length, another by its fineness, and others again as it chanced to be greasy, or lank, or curled. He would also blow on it with a bellows, to see how the parts arranged themselves: hold it near the fire, and watch the operation of its crisping by the heat: and although he had often been mistaken in his estimates of character, by the rules of his new science, he did not lose the confidence of his disciples on that account--some of them refusing to believe the truth, rather than to admit themselves mistaken; and others insisting that, if his science was not infallible, it very rarely deceived."

It was now our turn to submit our hands to Avarabet for examination. He discovered signs of the loftiest virtues and most heroic enterprise in the Brahmin; and, near the bottom of one of his nails, a deep-rooted sorrow, which would leave him only with his life. A transient shade of gloom on the Brahmin's countenance was soon succeeded by a piercing, inquisitive glance cast on the diviner. He saw the other's eyes directed on the miniature which he always wore, and which discovered itself to Avarabet as he stooped forward. A smile of contempt now took the place of his first surprise, and he seemed in a state of abstraction, during the continued rhapsodies of the oracle.

My hand was next examined; but little was said of me, except that I had been a great traveller, and should be so again; that I should encounter many dangers and difficulties; that I possessed more intelligence than sensibility, and more prudence than generosity. Thus he discovered in me great courage, enterprise, and constancy of purpose.

A hale, robust, well-set man, now bursting through the crowd, and thrusting out his hand, abruptly asked the wise man to tell him, if he could, in what part of the country he lived. Avarabet mentioned a distant district on the coast of Morosofia.

"Good," said the other; "and what is my calling?"

After a slight pause, he replied, that he got his living on the water.

"Good again. Shall I ever be rich?"

"No, not very:--never."

"Better and better," rejoined the inquirer, at the same time giving vent to a loud and hearty laugh. Surely, thought I, sailors are every where the same sort of beings, rough and boisterous as the elements they roam over.

"And what is your opinion of me farther?"

"You are bold, frank, improvident, credulous and good-natured."

"Excellent, indeed! Now, what will you say, old sham wisdom, when I tell you that I never made a voyage in my life; was never two days' journey from this spot, and am seldom off my own dominion? That I own the forest of Tongloo, where I sometimes hunt, from morning till night, and from night till morning, twelve out of the thirteen days in the year? That my wealth, which was considerable when I came to my estate, has, by my habits of life, greatly increased, and that I am bent upon adding to it yet more? I drink nothing but water; and have come here only to win a wager, that you were not as knowing as you pretended to be, and that I could impose on you. You thus have a specimen of my candour, improvidence, and credulity." So saying, he leaped on his zebra, gave a sort of huntsman's shout, and was off in a twinkling.

This adventure created great tumult in the crowd, a few enjoying the jest, but the greater number manifesting ill-will and resentment towards the sportsman. The

Brahmin and I took advantage of the confusion, to withdraw unnoticed by the by-standers. After remaining at our lodgings long enough to take rest and refreshment, and to make minutes of what we had seen, we proposed to spend the remainder of the night in the country, the weather being more pleasant at this time in that climate, than when the sun is above the horizon.

We accordingly set out when the earth was in her second quarter, and it was about two of our days before sunrise. After walking about three miles, the freshness of the morning air, the fragrance of the flowers, and the music of innumerable birds, whose unceasing carols testified their joy and delight at the approach of a more genial month, we came to a large, well cultivated farm, in which a number of coarse looking men were employed, with the aid of dogs, cross-bows, and other martial weapons, in hunting down llamas, and a small kind of buffalo, which, in one of our former walks, we had seen quietly feeding on a rich and extensive pasture. We inquired of some stragglers from the throng, the meaning of what we saw; but they were too much occupied with their sport to afford us any satisfaction. We walked on, indulging our imaginations in conjecture; but had not proceeded more than a quarter of a mile, before we beheld a similar scene going on to our left, by the same ill-looking crew. Our curiosity was now redoubled, and we resolved to wait a while on the highway, for the chance of some passenger more at leisure to answer our inquiries, and more courteously inclined than these fierce marauders. We had not stopped many minutes, before a well-dressed man, wearing the appearance of authority, having ridden up, we asked him to explain the cause of their violent, and seemingly lawless proceedings.

"You are strangers, I see, or you would have understood that I am exercising my baronial privilege of doing myself justice. These cattle belong to the owners of a neighbouring estate, by whom I and my tenants have been injured and insulted; and, according to the usage in such cases, I have given the signal to my people to lay hold on what they can of his flocks and herds, and, to quicken their exertions, I give them half of what they catch."

"And how does your neighbour bear this in the mean time?" said the Brahmin.

"Oh, for that matter," said the other, "he is not at all behindhand, and I lose nearly as many cattle as I get. But it gives me much more pleasure to kill one of his buffaloes or llamas, than it does pain me when he kills one of mine. I consider how much it will vex him, and that some of his vassals are thereby deprived of their sustenance. I have upwards of thirty strong men employed in ranging this plain and wood, and during the last year they took for me four hundred head."

"Indeed!--and how many did you lose in the same time?

"Not above three hundred and eighty."

"But very inferior?" said the Brahmin.

"Why, no," replied he: "as my pastures are richer and more luxuriant than his, two of my cattle are worth perhaps three of his."

"Is this custom," asked the Brahmin, "an advantage or a tax on your estate?"

"A tax, indeed! Why it is worth from four to five hundred head a-year."

"And how much is it worth to your neighbour?"

"I presume nearly as much."

"Do your vassals get rich by the bounty you give them?"

"As to that matter, some who are lucky succeed very well, and the rest make a living by it."

"And what do they give you for the privilege of hunting your neighbour's cattle?"

"Nothing at all: I even lose my customary rent from those who engage in it."

"And it is the same case with your neighbour?"

"Certainly," said he.

"Then," said the Brahmin, "it seems to me, if you would agree to lay aside this old custom, you would both be considerable gainers. I see you look incredulous, but listen a moment. Each one would, in that case, instead of having half his neighbour's cattle, have all his own; and, being kept in their native pastures, they would be less likely to stray away, and you could therefore slay and eat as you wanted them; whereas, in your hunting matches many more are either killed or maimed than are wanted for present use, and they are consequently consumed in waste. You would, moreover, be a gainer by the amount of the labour of these thirty boors, whom you keep in this employment, and who very probably acquire habits of ferocity, licentiousness, and waste, which are not very favourable to their obedience or fidelity."

The proprietor, having pondered a while upon my friend's remarks, in a tone of exultation said,--"Do you think, then, I could ever prevail on my people to forbear, when they saw a likely flock, from laying violent hands on it; or could I resist so favourable an opportunity of revenge? Nay, more; if we were then tamely to tie up our hands, do you think that Bulderent and his men would consent to do the same? No, no, old man," he continued, with great self-complacency, "your arguments appear plausible at first, but when closely considered, they will not stand the lest of experience. They are the fancies of a stranger--of one who knows more of theory than practice. Had you lived longer among us, you would have known that your ingenious project could never be carried into execution. If I observed it, Bulderent would not; and if he observed it, I verily believe I could not--and thus, you see, the thing is altogether impracticable." As one soon tires of preaching to the winds, the Brahmin contented himself with asking his new acquaintance to think more on the subject at his leisure; and we proceeded on our walk.

CHAPTER X.

The travellers visit a gentleman farmer, who is a great projector: his breed
of cattle: his apparatus for cooking: he is taken dangerously ill.

After we had gone about half a mile farther, our attention was arrested
by a gate of very singular character. It was extremely ingenious in its
structure, and, among other peculiarities, it had three or four latches,
for children, for grown persons, for those who were tall and those who
were short, and for the right hand as well as the left. In the act of opening, it was
made to crush certain berries, and the oil they yielded, was carried by a small duct
to the hinge, which was thus made to turn easily, and was prevented from creaking.
While we were admiring its mechanism, an elderly man, rather plainly dressed, on
a zebra in low condition, rode up, and showed that he was the owner of the mansion to which the gate belonged, and that he was not displeased with the curiosity
we manifested. We found him both intelligent and obliging. He informed us that
he was an experimental farmer; and when he learnt that we were strangers, and
anxious to inform ourselves of the state of agriculture in the country, he very civilly
invited us to take our next meal with him. Our walk having now made us hungry
and fatigued, we gladly accepted of his hospitality; whereupon he alighted, and
walked with us to his lodgings.

He was very communicative of his modes of cultivation and management, but
chiefly prided himself on his success in improving the size of his cattle. He informed
us that he had devoted sixteen years of his life to this object, and had then in his
farm-yard a buffalo nearly as heavy as three of the ordinary size. His practice was to
kill all the young animals which were not uncommonly large and thrifty; to cram
those he kept, with as much food as they would eat, and to tempt their appetites by

the variety of their nourishment, as well as of the modes of preparing it.

"All this," said he, "costs a great deal, it is true; but I am paid for it by the additional price." I was struck with this notable triumph of industry and skill in the goodly art of husbandry--that art which I venerate above every other; and I was all anxiety to receive from him some instructions which I might, in case I should have the good fortune to get safely back, communicate to my friends on Long-Island, who had never been able even to double the common size, and who boasted greatly of that: but a hesitating look, and a few inquiries on the part of my sly friend, checked my enthusiasm.

"Have you always," he asked, "had the same number of acres in grain and grass under your new and old system?"

"Pretty nearly," says the other. "My new breed, however, though fewer, consume more than their predecessors."

"How many head did you formerly sell in a year?"

"About thirty."

"How many do you now sell?"

"Though for some years I have not sold more than nine or ten, I expect to exceed that number in another year."

"Which you expect will yield you more than the thirty did formerly?"

"Certainly; because such meat as mine commands an extraordinary price."

"So long," replied the Brahmin, "as this is novelty, you may receive a part of the price which men are ever ready to pay for it; but as soon as others profit by your example, your meat falls to the ordinary rate, and then, if I understand you aright, as you will have somewhat less in quantity than you formerly had, your gross receipts will be less, to say nothing of your additional labour and expense."

"But who has the skill," quickly rejoined the other, "of which I can boast? and who would take the same trouble, although they had the skill?"

"But stop here a moment," said our host, "till I go to see how my last improved oil-cake is relished by my cattle."

The Brahmin then turning to me, said,--"This gentleman may, indeed, improve his fortune by the business of a grazier; but the same pains and unremitting attention would always be sure of a liberal reward, though the system on which they were exerted was not among the best. Nothing, my dear Atterley, is more true than the saying of your wise book--that all flesh is grass; and it always takes the same quantity of one to make a given quantity of the other, whether that given quantity may be in the form of a single individual, or two or three. But in the former case, great labour is required to force nature beyond her ordinary limits, and the same labour must be unceasingly kept up, or she will certainly relapse to her original dimensions. This system may do, as our host here tells us it actually does, for the moon, but it is not suited to our earth. If, however, you are ambitious of a name among the speculative men of your country, this little stone," added he, stooping, and picking up a small stone from the ground, "will answer your purpose quite as well as any improvement in husbandry. It is precisely of the same species as those which we threw over in our aerial voyages, and which, though correctly called moon-stones by the vulgar, (who are oftener right than the learned suppose,) some of the western philosophers declared to have been gravitated in the atmosphere."

"And is this really the origin," said I, "of that strange phenomenon, which has furnished so much matter of speculation to the sages both of Europe and America?"

"Nothing is more true," replied he. "These stones are common to the earth and to the moon; and some of those which have been so carefully analyzed by your most celebrated chemists, and pronounced different from any known mineral production of the earth, were small fragments of a very common rock in the mountains of Burma. In our first voyages we had taken some of them with us as ballast; and those which we first threw over, we afterwards learnt from the public journals, fell in France, some of the others fell in India, but the greater number in the ocean. Those which have fallen at other times, have been real fossils of the moon, and either such stones as this I hold in my hand, or such metallic substances as are repelled from that body, and attracted towards the earth; and it is the force with which they strike the earth, which first suggested the idea of a thunder-bolt.

"Our party were greatly amused at the disputations of a learned society in Europe, in which they undertook to give a mathematical demonstration that they could not be thrown from a volcano of the earth, nor from the moon, but were suddenly formed in the atmosphere. I should as soon believe that a loaf of bread could be made and baked in the atmosphere."

Finding that our landlord prided himself on his interior management, as well as on that without doors, we expressed a wish to see some of his household improvements. He readily consented, and conducted us at once into his kitchen, and showed us inventions and contrivances out of number, for saving fuel, and meat, and labour; in short, for saving every thing but money. The large room into which he carried us, appeared as a vast laboratory, from the infinite variety of pots, pans, skillets, knives, forks, ladles, mortars, sieves, funnels, and other utensils of metal, glass, pottery, and wood. The steam which he used for cooking, was carried along a pipe under a succession of kettles and boilers, descending in regular gradation, by which a great saving of fuel was effected; and, to perfect this part of the apparatus, the pipe could be removed, to give place to one of the size suited to the occasion.

His seven-guest pipe was now in use. The wood, which was all cut to the same length, and channelled out to admit the free passage of the air, was then duly placed in the stove, and set on fire; but the heat not passing very readily through all the sinuosities of the pipe, he ordered his head cook to screw on his exhauster. The man, in less than ten minutes, unscrewed a plate at the farther end, and fixed on an air-pump, made for the purpose, on which the door of the stove suddenly slammed to. Our host saw the accident, and hurrying to open the stove, fell over a heap of channelled logs, and cut a gash in his forehead. The cook ran to help him up; and after he was on his legs, and his forehead wiped, the stove was opened, when the fire, which had been deprived of its aliment, was entirely extinguished. I thought he was hardly sorry for the accident, as it afforded him an occasion of showing how ingeniously he kindled a fire. He had an electric machine brought to him, by means of which he set fire to a few grains of gunpowder; this lighted some tinder, which again ignited spirits, whose blaze reached the lower extremity of his lamp. Taking the precaution of keeping the stove open this time, the air was again exhausted at the farther end of the pipe, and in a little time the flame was seen to ascend even to the air-pump, and to scorch the parts made of wood; whereupon I saw a glow of triumph on his face, which amply compensated him for his wound and vexation. There was a grand machine for roasting, that carried the fire round the meat, the juices of which, he said, by a rotary motion, would be thrown to the surface, and either evaporate or be deteriorated. Here was also his digestor, for making soup of rams' horns, which he assured me contained a good deal of nourishment, and the only difficulty was in extracting it. He next showed us his smoke-retractor, which received the smoke near the top of the chimney, and brought it down to be burnt over again, by which he computed that he saved five cords and a half of wood in a year. The fire which dressed his victuals, pumped up, by means of a steam engine, water for the kitchen turned one or more spits, as well as two or three mills for grinding pepper, salt, &c.; and then, by a spindle through the wall, worked a churn in the dairy, and cleaned the knives: the forks, indeed, were still cleaned by hand; but he said he did not despair of effecting this operation in time, by machinery. I mentioned to him our contrivance of silver forks, to lessen this labour; but he coldly remarked, that he imagined science was in its infancy with us.

He informed us that he had been ten years in completing this ingenious machine; and certainly, when it was in full operation, I never saw exultation and delight so strongly depicted in any human face. The various sounds and sights, that met the ear and eye, in rapid succession, still farther worked on his feelings, and heightened his raptures. There was such a simmering, and hissing, and bubbling of boiled, and broiled, and fried--such a whirling, and jerking, and creaking of wheels, and cranks, and pistons--such clouds of steam, and vapours, and even smoke, notwithstanding all of the latter that was burnt,--that I almost thought myself in some great manufactory.

After having suffered as much as we could well bear, from the heat and confined air of this laboratory of eatables, and passed the proper number of compliments on the skill and ingenuity they displayed, we ascended to his hall, to partake of that feast, to prepare which we had seen all the elements and the mechanical powers called into action. There were a few of his city acquaintances present, besides ourselves: but whether it was owing to the effect of the steam from the dishes on our stomachs, or that this scientific cookery was not suited to our unpractised palates, I know not, but we all made an indifferent repast, except our host, who tasted every dish, and seemed to relish them all.

After sitting some time at table, conversing on the progress of science, its splendid achievements, and the pleasing prospects which it yet dimly showed in the future, our hospitable entertainer, perceiving we were fatigued with the labours of the day, invited us to take our next *lallaneae*, or sleep, with him, for which hospitality we felt very grateful. We were then shown to a room, in which there were marks of the same fertile invention, in saving labour and promoting convenience;

but we were too sleepy to take much notice of them. Our beds were filled with air, which is quite as good as feathers, except that when the leather covering gets a hole in it, from ripping, or other accidents, it loses its elasticity with its air--an accident which happened to me this very night; for a mouse having gnawed the leather where the housemaid's greasy fingers had left a mark, I sunk gently down, not to soft repose, but on the hard planks, where I uncomfortably lay until the bell warned us to rise for breakfast.

As soon as I was dressed, I walked out into a large garden, and, as the sun was not yet so high as to make it sultry, was enjoying the balmy sweetness of the air, and the flowering shrubs, which in beauty and fragrance almost exceeded those of India, when I saw a servant run by the garden wall, enter the stable, and bring out a zebra. On inquiring the cause, I was made to understand that our noble host was taken suddenly ill. I immediately returned to the house, and found the domestics running to and fro, and manifesting the greatest anxiety, as well as hurry, in their looks. I went into the Brahmin's room, and found him dressed. He went out, and after some time, informed me that our kind host had a violent *cholera morbus*, in consequence of the various kinds of food with which he had overloaded his stomach at dinner; that he considered himself near his last end, and was endeavouring to arrange his affairs for the event.

I could not help meditating on the melancholy uncertainty of human life, when I contrasted the comforts, the pleasures, the pride of conscious usefulness and genius felt by this gentleman a short time since, with the agony which that trying and bitter hour brings to the stoutest and most callous heart--when it must quit this state of being for another, of which it knows so little, and over which fear and doubt throw a gloom that hope cannot entirely dispel.

CHAPTER XI.

Lunarian physicians: their consultation--While they dispute the patient recovers--The travellers visit the celebrated teacher Lozzi Pozzi.

While I indulged in these sad meditations, and felt for my host while I felt no less for myself, I saw the physician approach who had been sent for. He was a tall, thin man, with a quick step, a lively, piercing eye, a sallow complexion, and very courteous manners, and always willing to display the ready flow of words for which he was remarkable. I felt great curiosity to witness the skill of this Lunar Aesculapius, and he was evidently pleased with the interest I manifested. It turned out that he was well acquainted with the Brahmin; and learning from the latter my wish, he conducted me into the room of our sick host. We found him lying on a straw bed, and strangely altered within a few hours. The physician, after feeling his pulse, (which, as every country has its peculiar customs, is done here about the temples and neck, instead of the wrist)-- after examining his tongue, his teeth, his water, and feces, proposed bleeding. We all walked to the door, and ventured to oppose the doctor's prescription, suggesting that the copious evacuations he had already experienced, might make bleeding useless, if not dangerous.

"How little like a man of sense you speak," said the other; "how readily you have chimed in with the prejudices of the vulgar! I should have expected better things from you: but the sway of empiricism is destined yet to have a long struggle before it receives its final overthrow. I have attacked it with success in many quarters; but when it has been prostrated in one place, it soon rises up in another. Have you, my good friend, seen my last essay on morbid action?"

The Brahmin replied, that he had not yet had an opportunity of meeting with it.

"I am sorry you have not," said the other. "I have there completely demonstrated that disease is an unit, and that it is the extreme of folly to divide diseases into classes, which tend but to produce confusion of ideas, and an unscientific practice. Sir," continued he, in a more animated tone, "there is a beautiful simplicity in this theory, which gives us assurance of its conformity to nature and truth. It needs but to be seen to be understood--but to be understood, to be approved, and carried into successful operation."

The Brahmin asked him if this unit did not present different symptoms on different occasions.

"Certainly," he replied: "from too much or too little action, in this set of vessels or that, it is differently modified, and must be treated accordingly."

"This unit, then," said my friend, "assumes different forms, and requires various remedies? Is there not, then, a convenience in separating these modifications (or *forms*, if you prefer it) from one another, by different names?"

"Stop, my friend; you do not apprehend the matter. I will explain." At this moment two other gentlemen, of a grave aspect and demeanour, entered the room. They also were physicians of great reputation in the city. They appeared to be formal and reserved towards one another, but they each manifested still more shyness and coldness towards the learned Shuro. They entered the sick chamber, and having informed themselves of the state of the patient, all three withdrew to a consultation.

They had not been long together, before their voices grew, from a whisper, so loud, that we could distinctly hear all they said. "Sir," says Dr. Shakrack, "the patient is in a state of direct debility: we must stimulate, if we would restore a healthy action. Pour in the *stimulantia* and *irritentia*, and my life for it, the patient is saved."

"Will you listen to me for one moment?" says Dr. Dridrano, the youngest of the three gentlemen. "It may be presumption for one of my humble pretensions to set myself in opposition to persons of your age, experience, and celebrity; but I am bound, by the sacred duties of the high functions I have undertaken to perform, to use my poor abilities in such a way as I can, to advance the noble science of medicine, and, in so doing, to give strength to the weak, courage to the disheartened, and comfort to the afflicted. Gentlemen, I say, I hope if my simple views should be found widely different from yours, you will not impute it to a presumption which is as foreign to my nature as it would be unsuited to your merits. I consider the human body a mere machine, whose parts are complicated, whose functions are various, and whose operations are liable to be impeded and frustrated by a variety of obstacles. There is, you know, one set of tubes, or vessels, for the blood; another for the lymph; another for the sweat; and so on. Now, although each of these fluids has its several channels, yet, if by any accident any one of them is obstructed, and there is so great an accumulation of the obstructed fluid that it cannot find vent by its natural channel, or duct, then you must carry off the redundancy by some other; for you well know, that that which can be carried off by one, can be carried off by all. Gentlemen, I beg you not to turn away; hear me for a moment. Then, if the current of the blood be obstructed, I make large draughts of urine, or sweat or saliva, or of the liquor amnii; and I find it matters little which of these evacuants I resort to. This system, to which, with deference to your longer experience, I have had the honour of giving some celebrity in Morosofia, explains how it is that such various remedies for the same disease have been in vogue at different times. They have all had in town able advocates. I could adduce undeniable testimonials of their efficacy, because, in fact, they are all efficacious; and it seems to me a mere matter of earthshine, whether we resort to one or the other mode of restoring the equilibrium of the human machine; all that we have to do, being to know when and to what extent it is proper to use either. Determine, then, gentlemen,--you, for whose maturer judgment and years I feel profound respect,--whether we shall blister, or sweat, or bleed, or salivate."

Dr. Shuro, who had manifested his impatience at this long harangue, by frequent interruptions, and which Dridrano's show of deference could scarcely keep down, hastily replied: "You have manifestly taken the hint of your theory from me; and because I have advanced the doctrine that disease is an unit, you come forward now, and insist that remedy is an unit too."

"You do me great honour, learned sir," said Dridrano. "Surely it would be very unbecoming, in one of my age and standing, to set up a theory in opposition to yours, but it would be yet more discreditable to be a plagiarist; and, with all due respect for your superior wisdom, it does seem to my feeble intellect, that no two theories can be more different. You use several remedies for one disease: I admit several diseases, and use one remedy."

"And does not darkness remind us of light," replied Shuro, "by the contrast? heat of cold--north of south?"

"Gentlemen," then said Shakrack, who had been walking to and fro, during the preceding controversy, "as you seem to agree so ill with each other, I trust you will unite in adopting my course. Let us begin with this cordial; we will then vary the stimulus, if necessary, by means of the elixir, and you will see the salutary effects immediately. A loss of blood would still farther increase the debility of the patient; and I appeal to your candour, Dr. Shuro, whether you ever practised venesection in such a case?"

"In such a case? ay, in what *you* would call much worse. I was not long since called in to a man in a dropsy. I opened a vein. He seemed from that moment to feel relief; and he so far recovered, that after a short time I bled him again. I returned the next day, and had I arrived half an hour sooner, I should have bled him a third time, and in all human probability have saved his life."

"If you had stimulated him, you might have had an opportunity of making your favourite experiment a little oftener," said Shakrack.

"You are facetious, sir; I imagine you have been using your own panacea some-what too freely to-day."

"Not so," said his opponent, angrily; "but if you are not more guarded in your expressions, I shall make use of yours, in a way you won't like."

Upon which they proceeded to blows, Dridrano all the while bellowing, "I beg, my worthy seniors, for the honour of science, that you will forbear!"

The noise of the dispute had waked the patient, who, learning the cause of the disturbance, calmly begged they would give themselves no concern about him, but let him die in peace. The domestics, who had been for some time listening to the dispute, on hearing the scuffle, ran in and parted the angry combatants, who, like an abscess just lanced, were giving vent to all the malignant humours that had been so long silently gathering.

In the mean while, the smooth and considerate Dr. Dridrano stept into the sick room, with the view of offering an apology for the unmannerly conduct of his brethren, and of tendering his single services, as the other sages of the healing art could not agree in the course to be pursued; when he found that the patient, profiting by the simple remedies of the Brahmin, and an hour's rest, had been so much refreshed, that he considered himself out of danger, and that he had no need of medical assistance; or, at any rate, he was unwilling to follow the prescriptions of one physician, which another, if not two others, unhesitatingly condemned. Each one then received his fee, and hurried home, to publish his own statement of the case in a pamphlet.

The Brahmin, who had never left the sick man's couch during his sleep, now that he was out of danger, was greatly diverted at the dispute. But he good-naturedly added, that, notwithstanding the ridiculous figure they had that day made, they were all men of genius and ability, but had done their parts injustice by their vanity, and the ambition of originating a new theory. "With all the extravagance," said he, "to which they push their several systems, they are not unsuccessful in practice, for habitual caution, and an instinctive regard for human life, which they never can extinguish, checks them in carrying their hypotheses into execution: and if I might venture to give an opinion on a subject of which I know so little, and there is so much to be known, I would say, that the most common error of theorists is to consider man as a machine, rather than an animal, and subject to one set of the laws of matter, rather than as subject to them all.

"Thus," he continued, "we have been regarded by one class of theorists as an hydraulic engine, composed of various tubes fitted with their several fluids, the laws and functions of which have been deduced from calculations of velocities, altitudes, diameters, friction, &c. Another class considered man as a mere chemical engine, and his stomach as an alembic. The doctrine of affinities, attractions, and repulsions, now had full play. Then came the notion of sympathies and antipathies, by which name unknown and unknowable causes were sought to be explained, and ignorance was cunningly veiled in mystery. But the science will never be in the right tract of improvement, until we consider, conjointly, the mechanical operations of the fluids, the chemical agency of the substances taken into the stomach, and the animal functions of digestion, secretion, and absorption, as evinced by actual observation." I told him that I believed that was now the course which was actually pursued in the best medical schools, both of Europe and America.

Our worthy host, though very feeble, had so far recovered as to dress himself, and receive the congratulations of his household, who had all manifested a concern for his situation, that was at once creditable to him and themselves. Expressing our gratitude for his kind attentions, and promising to renew our visit if we could, we bade him adieu.

We took a different road home from the way we had come, and had not walked far, before we met a number of small boys, each having a bag on his back, as large as he could stagger under. Surprised at seeing children of their tender years, thus prematurely put to severe labour, I was about to rail at the absurd custom of this strange country, when my friend checked me for my hasty judgment, and told me that these boys were on their way to school, after their usual monthly holiday. We attended them to their schoolhouse, which stood in sight, on the side of a steep chalky hill. The Brahmin told me that the teacher's name was Lozzi Pozzi, and that he had acquired great celebrity by his system of instruction. When the boys opened their bags, I found that instead of books and provisions, as I had expected, they were filled with sticks, which they told us constituted the arithmetical lessons they were required to practise at home. These sticks were of different lengths and dimensions, according to the number marked on them; so that by looking at the inscription, you could tell the size, or by seeing or feeling the size, you could tell the number.

The master now made his appearance, and learning our errand, was very communicative. He descanted on the advantages of this manual, and ocular mode of teaching the science of numbers, and gave us practical illustrations of its efficacy, by examining his pupils in our presence. He told the first boy he called up, and who did not seem to be more than seven or eight years of age, to add 5, 3, and 7 together, and tell him the result. The little fellow set about hunting, with great alacrity, over his bag, until he found a piece divided like three fingers, then a piece with five divisions, and lastly, one with seven, and putting them side by side, he found the piece of a correspondent length, and thus, in less than eight minutes and a half, answered, "fifteen." The ingenious master then exercised another boy in subtraction, and a third in multiplication: but the latter was thrown into great confusion, for one of the pieces having lost a division, it led him to a wrong result.

The teacher informed us that he taught geometry in the same way, and had even extended it to grammar, logic, rhetoric, and the art of composition. The rules of syntax were discovered by pieces of wood, interlocking with each other in squares, dovetails, &c., after the manner of geographical cards; and as they chanced to fit together, so was the concordance between the several parts of speech ascertained. The machine for composition occupied a large space; different sets of synonymes were arranged in compartments of various sizes. When the subject was familiar, a short piece was used; when it was stately or heroic, then the longest slips that could be found were resorted to. Those that were rounded at the ends were mellifluous; the jagged ones were harsh; the thick pieces expressed force and vigour. Where the curves corresponded at one end, they served for alliteration; and when at the other, they answered for rhyme. By way of proving its progress, he showed us a composition by a man who was deaf and dumb, in praise of Morosofia, who, merely by the use of his eyes and hands, had made an ingenious and high-sounding piece of eloquence, though I confess that the sense was somewhat obscure. We went away filled with admiration for the great Lozzi Pozzi's inventions.

Having understood that there was an academy in the neighbourhood, in which youths of maturer years were instructed in the fine arts, we were induced to visit it; but there being a vacation at that time, we could see neither the professors nor students, and consequently could gain little information of the course of discipline and instruction pursued there. We were, however, conducted to a small *menagerie* attached to the institution, by its keeper, where the habits and accomplishments of the animals bore strong testimony in favour of the diligence and skill of their teachers.

We there saw two game-cocks, which, so far from fighting, (though they had been selected from the most approved breed,) billed and cooed like turtle-doves. There was a large zebra, apparently ill-tempered, which showed his anger by running at and butting every animal that came in his way. Two half-grown llamas, which are naturally as quiet and timid as sheep, bit each other very furiously, until they foamed at the mouth. And, lastly, a large mastiff made his appearance, walking in a slow, measured gait, with a sleek tortoise-shell cat on his back; and she, in turn, was surmounted by a mouse, which formed the apex of this singular pyramid.

The keeper, remarking our unaffected surprise at the exhibition, asked us if we could now doubt the unlimited force of education, after such a display of the triumph of art over nature. While he was speaking, the mastiff, being jostled by the two llamas still awkwardly worrying each other, turned round so suddenly, that the mouse was dislodged from his lofty position, and thrown to the ground; on seeing which, the cat immediately sprang upon it, with a loud purring noise, which being heard by the dog, he, with a fierce growl, suddenly seized the cat. The llamas, alarmed at this terrific sound, instinctively ran off, and having, in their flight, approached the heels of the zebra, he gave a kick, which killed one of them on the spot.

The keeper, who was deeply mortified at seeing the fabric he had raised with such indefatigable labour, overturned in a moment, protested that nothing of the sort had ever happened before. To which we replied, by way of consolation, that perhaps the same thing might never happen again; and that, while his art had achieved a conquest over nature, this was only a slight rebellion of nature against art. We then thanked him for his politeness, and took our leave.

CHAPTER XII.

Election of the Numnoonce, or town-constable--Violence of parties--Singular institution of the Syringe Boys--The prize-fighters--Domestic manufactures.

When we got back to the city, we found an unusual stir and bustle among the citizens, and on inquiring the cause, we understood they were about to elect the town-constable. After taking some refreshment at our lodgings, where we were very kindly received, we again went out, and were hurried along with the crowd, to a large building near the centre of the city. The multitude were shouting and hallooing with great vehemence. The Brahmin remarking an elderly man, who seemed very quiet in the midst of all this ferment, he thought him a proper person to address for information.

"I suppose," says he, "from the violence of these partisans, they are on different sides in religion or politics?"

"Not at all," said the other; "those differences are forgotten at the present, and the ground of the dispute is, that one of the candidates is tall, and the other is short--one has a large foretop, and the other is bald. Oh, I forgot; one has been a schoolmaster, and the other a butcher."

Curiosity now prompted me to enter into the thickest of the throng; and I had never seen such fury in the maddest contests between old George Clinton and Mr. Jay, or De Witt Clinton and Governor Tompkins, in my native State. They each reproached their adversaries in the coarsest language, and attributed to them the vilest principles and motives. Our guide farther told us that the same persons, with two others, had been candidates last year, when the schoolmaster prevailed; and, as the supporters of the other two unsuccessful candidates had to choose now between the remaining two, each party was perpetually reproaching the other with inconsistency. A dialogue between two individuals of opposite sides, which we happened to hear, will serve as a specimen of the rest.

"Are you not a pretty fellow to vote for Bald-head, whom you have so often called rogue and blockhead?"

"It becomes you to talk of consistency, indeed! Pray, sir, how does it happen that you are now against him, when you were so lately sworn friends, and used to eat out of the same dish?"

"Yes; but I was the butcher's friend too. I never abused him. You'll never catch me supporting a man I have once abused."

"But I catch you abusing the man you once supported, which is rather worse. The difference between us is this:--you professed to be friendly to both; I professed to be hostile to both: you stuck to one of your friends, and cast the other off; and I acted the same towards my enemies." A crowd then rushed by, crying "Huzza for the Butcher's knives! Damn pen and ink--damn the books, and all that read in them! Butchers' knives and beef for ever!"

We asked our guide what these men were to gain by the issue of the contest.

"Nineteenths of them nothing. But a few hope to be made deputies, if their candidates succeed, and they therefore egg on the rest."

We drew near to the scaffold where the candidates stood, and our ears were deafened with the mingled shouts and exclamations of praise and reproach. "You cheated the corporation!" says one. "You killed two black sheep!" says another. "You can't read a warrant!" "You let Dondon cheat you!" "You tried to cheat Nincan!" "You want to build a watch-house!" "You have an old ewe at home now, that you did not come honestly by!" "You denied your own hand!"--with other ribaldry still more gross and indecent. But the most singular part of the scene was a number of little boys, dressed in black and white, who all wore badges of the parties to which they belonged, and were provided with a syringe, and two canteens, one filled with rose-water, and the other with a black liquid, of a very offensive smell, the first of which they squirted at their favourite candidates and voters, and the last on those of the opposite party. They were drawn up in a line, and seemed to be under regular discipline; for, whenever the captain of the band gave the word, "Vilti Mindoc!" they discharged the dirty liquid from their syringes; and when he said "Vilti Goulgoul!" they filled the air with perfume, that was so overpowering as sometimes to produce sickness. The little fellows would, between whiles, as if to keep their hands in, use the black squirts against one another; but they often gave them a dash of the rose-water at the same time.

I wondered to see men submit to such indignity; but was told that the custom had the sanction of time; that these boys were brought up in the church, and were regularly trained to this business. "Besides," added my informer, "the custom is not without its use; for it points out the candidates at once to a stranger, and especially him who is successful, those being always the most blackened who are the most popular." But it was amusing to see the ludicrous figure that the candidates and some of the voters made. If you came near them on one side, they were like roses dripping with the morning dew; but on the other, they were as black as chimney sweeps, and more offensive than street scavengers. As these Syringe Boys, or Goulmins, are thus protected by custom, the persons assailed affected to despise them; but I could ever and anon see some of the most active partisans clapping them on the back, and saying, "Well done, my little fellows! give it to them again! You shall have a ginger-cake--and you shall have a new cap," &c. Surely, thought I, our custom of praising and abusing our public men in the newspapers, is far more rational than this. After the novelty of the scene was over, I became wearied and disgusted with their coarseness, violence, and want of decency, and we left them without waiting to see the result of the contest.

In returning to our lodgings, the Brahmin took me along a quarter of the town in which I had never before been. In a little while we came to a lofty building, before the gate of which a great crowd were assembled. "This," said my companion, "is one of the courts of justice." Anxious to see their modes of proceeding in court, I pushed through the crowd, followed by the Brahmin, and on entering the building, found myself in a spacious amphitheatre, in the middle of which I beheld, with surprise, several men engaged, hand to hand, in single combat. On asking an explanation of my friend, he informed me that these contests were favourite modes of settling private disputes in Morosofia: that the prize-fighters I saw, hired themselves to any one who conceived himself injured in person, character, or property. "It seems a strange mode of settling legal disputes," I remarked, "which determines a question in favour of a party, according to the strength and wind of his champion."

"Nor is that all," said the Brahmin, "as the judges assign the victory according to certain rules and precedents, the reasons of which are known only to themselves, if known at all, and which are often sufficiently whimsical--as sometimes a small scratch in the head avails more than a disabling blow in the body. The blows too, must be given in the right time, as well as in the right place, or they pass for nothing. In short, of all those spectators who are present to witness the powers and address of the prize-fighters, not one in a hundred can tell who has gained the victory, until the judges have proclaimed it."

"I presume," said I, "that the champions who thus expose their persons and lives in the cause of another, are Glonglims?"

"There," said he, "you are altogether mistaken. In the first place, the prize-fighters seldom sustain serious injury. Their weapons do not endanger life; and as each one knows that his adversary is merely following his vocation, they often fight without animosity. After the contest is over, you may commonly see the combatants walking and talking very sociably together: but as this circumstance makes them a little suspected by the public, they affect the greater rage when in conflict, and occasionally quarrel and fight in downright earnest. No," he continued, "I am told it is a very rare thing to see one of these prize-fighters who is a Glonglim; but most of their employers belong to this unhappy race."

On looking more attentively, I perceived many of these beings among the spectators, showing, by their gestures, the greatest anxiety for the issue of the contest. They each carried a scrip, or bag, the contents of which they ever and anon gave to their respective champions, whose wind, it is remarked, is very apt to fail, unless thus assisted.

Having learnt some farther particulars respecting this singular mode of litigation, which would be uninteresting to the general reader, I took my leave, not without secretly congratulating myself on the more rational modes in which justice is administered on earth.

When we had nearly reached our lodgings, we heard a violent altercation in the house, and on entering, we found our landlord and his wife engaged in a dispute respecting their domestic economy, and they both made earnest appeals to my companion for the correctness of their respective opinions. The old man was in favour of their children making their own shoes and clothes; and his wife insisted that it would be better for them to stick to their garden and dairy, with the proceeds of which they could purchase what they wanted. She asserted that they could readily sell all the fruits and vegetables they could raise; and that whilst they would acquire greater skill by an undivided attention to one thing, they who followed the business of tailors, shoemakers, and seamstresses, would, in like manner, become more skil-ful in their employments, and consequently be able to work at a cheaper rate. She farther added, that spinning and sewing were unhealthy occupations; they would give the girls the habit of stooping, which would spoil their shapes; and that their thoughts would be more likely to be running on idle and dangerous fancies, when sitting at their needles, than when engaged in more active occupations.

This dame was a very fluent, ready-witted woman, and she spoke with the confidence that consciousness of the powers of disputation commonly inspires. She went on enlarging on the mischiefs of the practice she condemned, and, by insen-sible gradations, so magnified them, that at last she clearly made out that there was no surer way of rendering their daughters sickly, deformed, vicious, and unchaste, than to set them about making their own clothes.

After she had ceased, (which she did under a persuasion that she had anticipat-ed and refuted every argument that could be urged in opposition to her doctrine,) the husband, with an emotion of anger that he could not conceal, began to defend his opinion. He said, as to the greater economy of his plan, there could be no doubt; for although they might, at particular times, make more by gardening than they could save by spinning or sewing, yet there were other times when they could not till the ground, and when, of course, if they did not sew or spin, they would be idle; but if they did work, the proceeds would be clear gain. He said he did not wish his daughters to be constantly employed in making clothes, nor was it necessary that they should be. A variety of other occupations, equally indispensable, claimed their attention, and would leave but a comparatively small portion of time for needle-work: that in thus providing themselves with employment at home, they at least saved the time of going backwards and forwards, and were spared some trips to market, for the sale of vegetables to pay, as would then be necessary, for the work done by others. Besides, the tailor who was most convenient to them, and who, it was admitted, was a very good one, was insolent and capricious; would sometimes extort extravagant prices, or turn them into ridicule; and occasionally went so far as to set his water-dogs upon them, of which he kept a great number. He declared, that for his part he would incur a little more expense, rather than he would be so imposed upon, and subjected to so much indignity and vexation.

He denied that sewing would affect his daughters' health, unless, perhaps, they followed it exclusively as an occupation; but, as they would have it in their power to consult their inclinations and convenience in this matter, they might take it up when the occasion required, and lay it down whenever they found it irksome or fatiguing: that as they themselves were inclined to follow this course, it was a plain proof that the occupation was not unhealthy. He maintained that they would stoop just as much in gardening, and washing and nursing their children, as in sewing; and that we were not such frail or unpliant machines as to be seriously injured, unless we persisted in one set of straight, formal notions, but that we were adapted to variety, and were benefited by it. That as to the practice being favourable to wantonness and vice, while he admitted that idleness was productive of these effects, he could not see how one occupation encouraged them more than another. That the tailor, for example, whom he had been speaking of, though purse-proud, overbearing, and rapacious, was not more immoral or depraved than his neighbours, and had probably less of the libertine than most of them. He admitted that evil thoughts would enter the mind in any situation, and could not reasonably be expected to be kept out of his daughters' heads (being, as he said, but women): yet he conceived such a result as far less probable, if they were suffered to ramble about in the streets, and to chaffer with their customers, than if they were kept to sedate and diligent employment at home.

Having, with great warmth and earnestness, used these arguments, he concluded, by plainly hinting to his wife that she had always been the apologist of the tailor, in all their disputes; and that she could not be so obstinately blind to the irrefragable reasoning he had urged, if she were not influenced by her old hankering after this fellow, and did not consult his interests in preference to those of her own family. Upon this remark the old woman took fire, and, in spite of our presence, they both had recourse to direct and the coarsest abuse.

The Brahmin did not, as I expected, join me in laughing at the scene we had just witnessed; but, after some musing, observed: "There is much truth in what each of these parties say. I blame them only for the course they take towards each other. Their dispute is, in fact, of a most frivolous and unmeaning character; for, if the father was to carry his point, the girls would occasionally sell the productions of their garden, and pay for making their clothes, or even buy them ready made. Were the mother, on the other hand, to prevail, they would still occasionally use their needles, and exercise their taste and skill in sewing, spinning, knitting, and the like. Nay," added he, "if you had not been so much engrossed with this angry and indecorous altercation, you might have seen two of them at their needles, in an adjoining apartment, while one was busy at work in the garden, and another up to the elbows in the soap-suds--all so closely engaged in their several pursuits, that they hardly seemed to know they were the subject of discussion."

I told the Brahmin that a dispute, not unlike this, had taken place in my own country, a few years since; some of our politicians contending that agricultural labour was most conducive to the national wealth, whilst others maintained that manufacturing industry was equally advantageous, wherever it was voluntarily pursued;--but that the controversy had lately assumed a different character--the question now being, not whether manufactures are as beneficial as agriculture, but whether they deserve extraordinary encouragement, by taxing those who do not give them a preference.

"That is," said the Brahmin, "as if our landlady, by way of inducing her daughters to give up gardening for spinning, were to tell them, if they did not find their new occupation as profitable as the old, she would more than make up the difference out of her own pocket, which, though it might suit the daughters very well, would be a losing business to the family."

CHAPTER XIII.

Description of the Happy Valley--The laws, customs, and manners of the Okalbians--Theory of population--Rent--System of government.

The Brahmin, who was desirous of showing me what was most remarkable in this country, during the short time we intended to stay, thought this a favourable time to visit Okalbia, or the Happy Valley. The Okalbians are a tribe or nation, who live separated from the rest of the Lunar world, and whose wise government, prudence, industry, and integrity, are very highly extolled by all, though, by what I can learn, they have few imitators. They dwell about three hundred miles north of the city of Alamatua, in a fertile valley, which they obtained by purchase about two hundred years since, and which is about equal to twenty miles square, that is, to four hundred square miles. A carriage and four well-broke dogs, was procured for us, and we soon reached the foot of the mountain that encloses the fortunate valley, in about fifty-two hours. We then ascended, for about three miles, with far fatigue than I formerly experienced in climbing the Catskill mountains of my native State, and found ourselves on the summit of an extensive ridge, which formed the margin of a vast elliptical basin, the bottom of which presented a most beautiful landscape. The whole surface was like a garden, interspersed with patches of wood, clumps of trees, and houses standing singly or in groupes. A lake, about a mile across, received several small streams, and on its edge was a town, containing about a thousand houses. After enjoying the beauties of the scene for some minutes, we descended by a rough winding road, and entered this Lunar Paradise, in about four hours. Along the sides of the highway we travelled, were planted rows of trees, not unlike our sycamores, which afforded a refreshing shade to the traveller; and commonly a rivulet ran bubbling along one side or the other of the road.

After journeying about eight miles, we entered a neat, well built town, which contained, as we were informed, about fifteen thousand inhabitants. The Brahmin informed me, that in a time of religious fervour, about two centuries ago, a charter was granted to the founder of a new sect, the Volbins, who had chanced to make converts of some of the leading men in Morosofia, authorising him and his followers to purchase this valley of the hunting tribe to whom it belonged, and to govern themselves by their own laws. They found no difficulty in making the purchase. It was then used as a mere hunting ground, no one liking to settle in a place that seemed shut out from the rest of the world. At first, the new settlers divided the land equally among all the inhabitants, one of their tenets being, that as there was no difference of persons in the next world, there should be no difference in sharing the good things of this. They tried at first to preserve this equality; but finding it impracticable, they abandoned it. It is said that after about thirty years, by reason of a difference in their industry and frugality, and of some families spending less than they made, and some more, the number of land owners was reduced to four hundred, and that fifty of these held one half of the whole; since which time the number of landed proprietors has declined with the population, though not in the same proportion. As the soil is remarkably fertile, the climate healthy, and the people temperate and industrious, they multiplied very rapidly until they reached their present numbers, which have been long stationary, and amount to 150,000, that is, about four hundred to a square mile; of these, more than one half live in towns and villages, containing from one hundred to a thousand houses.

They have little or no commerce with any other people, the valley producing every vegetable production, and the mountains every mineral, which they require; and in fact, they have no foreign intercourse whatever, except when they visit, or are visited from curiosity. Though they have been occasionally bullied and threatened by lawless and overbearing neighbours; yet, as they can be approached by only a single gorge in the mountain, which is always well garrisoned, (and they present no sufficient object to ambition, to compensate for the scandal of invading so inoffensive and virtuous a people,) they have never yet been engaged in war.

I felt very anxious to know how it was that their numbers did not increase, as they were exempt from all pestilential diseases, and live in such abundance, that a beggar by trade has never been known among them, and are remarkable for their moral habits.

"Let us inquire at the fountain-head," said the Brahmin; and we went to see the chief magistrate, who received us in a style of unaffected frankness, which in a moment put us at our ease. After we had explained to him who we were, and answered such inquiries as he chose to make:

"Sir," said I, through the Brahmin, who acted as interpreter, "I have heard much of your country, and I find, on seeing it, that it exceeds report, in the order, comfort, contentment, and abundance of the people. But I am puzzled to find out how it is that your numbers do not increase. I presume you marry late in life?"

"On the contrary," said he; "every young man marries as soon as he receives his education, and is capable of managing the concerns of a family. Some are thus qualified sooner, and some later."

"Some occasionally migrate, then?"

"Never. A number of our young men, indeed, visit foreign countries, but not one in a hundred settles abroad."

"How, then, do your associates continue stationary?"

"Nothing is more easy. No man has a larger family than his land or labour can support, in comfort; and as long as that is the case with every individual, it must continue to be the case with the whole community. We leave the matter to individual discretion. The prudential caution which is thus indicated, has been taught us by our own experience. We had gone on increasing, under the encouraging influence of a mild system of laws, genial climate, and fruitful soil, until, about a century ago, we found that our numbers were greater than our country, abundant as it is, could comfortably support; and our seasons being unfavourable for two successive years, many of our citizens were obliged to banish themselves from Okalbia; and their education not fitting them for a different state of society, they suffered severely, both in their comforts and morals. It is now a primary moral duty, enforced by all our juvenile instructors with every citizen, to adapt his family to his means; and thus a regard which each individual has for his offspring, is the salvation of the State."

"And can these prudential restraints be generally practised? What a virtuous people! Love for one another brings the two sexes together--love for their offspring makes them separate!"

"I see," said the magistrate, smiling, "you are under an error. No separation takes place, and none is necessary."

"How, then, am I to believe.....?"

"You are to believe nothing," said he, with calm dignity, "which is incompatible with virtue and propriety. I see that the most important of all sciences--that one on which the well-being and improvement of society mainly depends,--is in its infancy with you. But whenever you become as populous as we are, and unite the knowledge of real happiness with the practice of virtue, you will understand it. It is one of our maxims, that heaven gives wisdom to man in such portions as his situation requires it; and no doubt it is the same with the people of your earth."

I did not, after this, push my inquiries farther; but remarked, aside to the Brahmin,--"I would give a good deal to know this secret, provided it would suit our planet."

"It is already known there," replied he, "and has been long practised by many in the east: but in the present state of society with you, it might do more harm than good to be made public, by removing one of the checks of licentiousness, where women are so unrestrained as they are with you."

Changing now the subject, I ventured to inquire how they employed their leisure hours, and whether many did not experience here a wearisome sameness, and a feeling of confinement and restraint.

"It is true," said the magistrate, "men require variety; but I would not have you suppose he cannot find it here. He may cultivate his lands, improve his mind, educate his children; these are his serious occupations, affording every day some employment that is, at once, new and interesting: and, by way of relaxation, he has music, painting, and sculpture; sailing, riding, conversation, storytelling, and reading the news of what is passing, both in the valley and out of it."

I asked if they had newspapers. He answered in the affirmative; and added, that they contained minute details of the births, deaths, marriages, accidents, state of the weather and crops, arbitrations, public festivals, inventions, original poetry, and prose compositions. In addition to which, they had about fifty of their most promising young men travelling abroad, who made observations on all that was remarkable in the countries they passed through, which they regularly transmitted once a month to Okalbia. I inquired if they travelled at the public expense or their own?

"They always pursue some profession or trade, by the profits of which they support themselves. We have nothing but intellect and ingenuity to export; for though our country produces every thing, there is no commodity that we can so well spare. Their talents find them employment every where; and the necessity they are under of a laborious exertion of these talents, and of submitting to a great deal from those whose customs and manners are not to their taste, and whom they feel inferior to themselves, is a considerable check to the desire to go abroad, so much so, that we hold out the farther inducement of political distinction when they return."

"What, then! you have ambition among you?"

"Certainly; our institutions have only tempered it, and not vainly endeavoured to extinguish it; and we find it employment in this way: Of our youthful travellers, those who are most diligent in their vocation; who give the most useful information, and communicate it in the happiest manner, are made magistrates, on their return, and sometimes have statues decreed to them. Besides, the name which their conduct or talents procure them abroad, is echoed back to the valley, long before their return, and has much influence in the general estimate of their character.

"But have you not many more competitors, than you have public offices?"

"There are, without doubt, many who desire office; but to manifest their wish, would be one of the surest means of defeating it. We require modesty, (at least in appearance,) moderation and disinterestedness, and of course, the less pains a candidate takes to show himself off, the better."

"But have they no friends, who can at once render them this service, and relieve them from the odium of it?"

"There is, indeed, somewhat of this; but you must remember, that the highest of our magistrates has comparatively little power. He has no army, no treasury, no patronage; he merely executes the laws. But, as a farther check on the immoderate zeal of friends, the expense of doing this, as well as of maintaining him in office, is defrayed by those who vote for him. There seems, at first view, but little justice in this regulation; but we think, that as every one cannot have his way, those who carry their point, and have the power, should also bear the burden: besides, in this way the voices of the most generous and disinterested prevail. We have," he added, "found this the most difficult part of our government. We once thought that the very lively interest excited in the electioneering contests, particularly for that of Gompoo, or chief magistrate, was to be ascribed to the power he possessed; and we resorted to various expedients to lessen it--such as dividing it among a greater number--requiring a quick rotation of office--abridging the powers themselves: but we discovered, that however small the power, the distinction it gave to those who possessed it, was always an object of lively interest with the ambitious, and indeed with the public in general. We have, therefore, enlarged the power, and the term of holding it, and make him who would attain it, purchase it by previous exertion and self-denial: and we farther compel those who favour him, to lose as well as gain. We array the love of money against the love of power; or rather, one love of power to another. Moreover, as it is only by the civic virtues that our citizens recommend themselves to popular favour, there is nothing of that enthusiasm which military success excites among the natives."

Our Washington then presented himself to my mind, and for a moment I began to question his claim to the unexampled honours bestowed on him by his countrymen, until I recollected that he was as distinguished by his respect for the laws, and his sound views of national policy, as for his military services.

I then inquired into the occupations and condition of those who were without land; and was told that they were either cultivators of the soil, or practised some liberal or mechanical art; and, partly owing to the education they receive, and partly from the active competition that exists among them, they are skilful, diligent, and honest. Now and then there are some exceptions, according to the proverb, that *in the best field of grain there will be some bad ears*. The landowners sometimes cultivate the soil with their own hands--sometimes with hired labourers--and sometimes they rent them for about a third of their produce. The smallest proprietors commonly adopt the first course; the middling, the second; and the great landholders the third."

"But I thought," said I, "that all the land in the valley was of equal fertility."

"So it is; but what has that to do with rent?"

"Sir," said I, "our ablest writers on this subject have lately discovered that there can be no rent where there is not a gradation of soils, such as exists in every country of the earth."

"I see not," said he, "what could have led them into that error. It is true, if there was inferior land, there would be a difference of rent in proportion to the difference of fertility; and if it was so poor as merely to repay the expense of cultivation, it would yield no rent at all. But surely, if one man makes as much as several consume, (and this he can easily do with us,) he will be able to get much of their labour in exchange for this surplus, which is so indispensable to them, and to get more and more, until the greatest number has come into existence which such surplus can support. What they thus give, if the proprietor retains the land himself, you may regard as the extraordinary profits of agricultural labour, or rent, if paid to any one to whom he transfers this benefit. This is precisely our present situation."

There was no denying this statement of facts: but I could not help exclaiming,--"Surely there is nothing certain in the universe; or rather, truth is one thing in the moon, and another thing on the earth."

CHAPTER XIV.

Farther account of Okalbia--The Field of Roses--Curious superstition concerning that flower--The pleasures of smell traced to association, by a Glonglim philosopher.

Though I felt some reluctance to abuse the patience of this polite and intelligent magistrate, I could not help making some inquiry about the jurisprudence of his country, and first, what was their system of punishment.

"We have no capital punishment," says he; "for, from all we learn, it is not more efficacious in preventing crime, than other punishments which are milder; and we prefer making the example to offenders a lasting one. But we endeavour to prevent offences, not so much by punishment as by education; and the few crimes committed among us, bring certain censure on those who have the early instruction of the criminal. Murders are very rare with us; thefts and robbery perhaps still more so. Our ordinary disputes about property, are commonly settled by arbitration, where, as well as in court, each party is permitted to state his case, to examine what witnesses and to ask what questions he pleases."

"You do not," said I, "examine witnesses who are interested?"

"Why not? The judges even examine the parties themselves."

I then told him that the smallest direct interest in the issue of the controversy, disqualified a witness with us, from the strong bias it created to misrepresent facts, and even to misconceive them.

He replied with a smile,--"It seems to me that your extreme fear of hearing falsehood, must often prevent you from ascertaining the truth. It is true, that wherever the interest of a witness is involved, it has an immediate tendency to make him misstate facts: but so would personal ill-will--so would his sympathies--so would any strong feeling. What, then, is your course in these cases?"

I told him that these objections applied to the credibility, and not to the competency, of witnesses, which distinctions of the lawyers I endeavoured to explain to him.

"Then I think you often exclude a witness who is under a small bias, and admit another who is under a great one. You allow a man to give testimony in a case in which the fortune or character of his father, brother or child is involved, but reject him in a case in which he is not interested to the amount of a greater sum than he would give to the first beggar he met. Is it not so?"

"That, indeed, may be the operation of the rule. But cases of such flagrant inconsistency are very rare; and this rule, like every other, must be tried by its general, and not its partial effects."

"True; but your rule must at least be a troublesome one, and give rise to a great many nice distinctions, that make it difficult in the application. All laws are sufficiently exposed to this evil, and we do not wish unnecessarily to increase it. We have, therefore, adopted the plan of allowing either party to ask any question of any witness he pleases, and leave it to the judges to estimate the circumstances which may bias the witness. We, in short, pursue the same course in investigating facts in court that we pursue out of it, when no one forms a judgment until he has first heard what the parties and their friends say on the subject."

On my return home, I repeated this conversation to a lawyer of my acquaintance, who told me that such a rule of evidence might do for the people in the moon, but it certainly would not suit us. I leave the matter to be settled by more competent heads than mine, and return to my narrative.

I farther learnt from this intelligent magistrate, that the territory of the Happy Valley, or Okalbia, is divided into forty-two counties, and each county into ten districts. In each district are three magistrates, who are appointed by the legislature. Causes of small value are decided by the magistrates of the district; those of greater importance, by the county courts, composed of all the magistrates of the ten districts; a few by the court of last court, consisting of seven judges. The legislature consists of two houses, of which the members are elected annually, three from each county for one branch, and one member for the other. No qualification of property is required either to vote, or to be eligible to either house of the legislature, as they believe that the natural influence of property is sufficient, without adding to that influence by law; and that the moral effects of education among them, together with a few provisions in their constitution, are quite sufficient to guard against any improper combination of those who have small property. Besides, there are no odious privileges exclusively possessed by particular classes of men, to excite the envy or resentment of the other classes, and induce them to act in concert.

"Have you, then, no parties?" said I.

"Oh yes; we are not without our political parties and disputes; and we sometimes wrangle about very small matters--such as, what amount of labour shall be bestowed on the public roads--the best modes of conducting our schools and colleges--the comparative merits of the candidates for office, or the policy of some proposed change in the laws. Man is made, you know, of very combustible materials, and may be kindled as effectually by a spark falling at the right time, in the right place, as when within reach of a great conflagration."

The women appeared here to be under few restraints. I understood that they were taught, like our sex, all the speculative branches of knowledge, but that they were more especially instructed, by professed teachers, in cookery, needlework, and every sort of domestic economy; as were the young men in the occupations which require strength and exposure. They have a variety of public schools, and some houses for public festivals, but no public hospitals or almshouses whatever, the few cases of private distress or misfortune being left for relief to the merits of the sufferer and the compassion of individuals.

After passing a week among this singular and fortunate people, whom we every where found equally amiable, intelligent, and hospitable, we returned to Alamatua in the same way that we had come; that is, in a light car, drawn by four large mastiffs. When we had recovered from the fatigues of the journey, and I had carefully committed to paper all that I had learnt of the Okalbians, the Brahmin and I took a walk towards a part of the suburbs which I had not yet seen, and where some of the literati of his acquaintance resided. The sun appeared to be not more than two hours high (though, in fact, it was more than fifty); the sky was without a cloud, and a fresh breeze from the mountains contributed to make it like one of the most delightful summer evenings of a temperate climate.

We carelessly rambled along, enjoying the balmy freshness of the air, the picturesque scenery of the neighbouring mountains, the beauty or fragrance of some vegetable productions, and the oddity of others, until, having passed through a thick wood, we came to an extensive plain, which was covered with rose-bushes. The queen of flowers here appeared under every variety of colour, size, and species--red, white, black, and yellow--budding, full-blown, and half-blown;--some with thorns, and some without; some odourless, and others exhaling their unrivalled perfume with an overpowering sweetness. I was about to pluck one of these flowers, (of which I have always been particularly fond,) when a man, whom I had not previously observed, stepping up behind me, seized my arm, and asked me if I knew what I was doing. He told us that the roses of this field, which is called Gulgal, were deemed sacred, and were not allowed to be gathered without the special permission of the priests, under a heavy penalty; and that he was one of those whose duty it was to prevent the violation of the law, and to bring the offenders to punishment.

The Brahmin, having diverted himself a while with my surprise and disappointment, then informed me, that the rose had ever been regarded in Morosofia, as the symbol of female purity, delicacy, and sweetness; which notion had grown into a popular superstition, that whenever a marriage is consummated on the earth, one of these flowers springs up in the moon; and that in colour, shape, size, or other property, it is a fit type of the individual whose change of state is thus commemorated.

"What, father," said I, "could have given rise to so strange an opinion?"

"I know not," said he; "but I have heard it thus explained:--That the roses generally spring up, as well as blow, in the course of their long nights, during which the earth's resplendent disc is the most conspicuous object in the heavens; which two facts stand, in the opinion of the multitude, in the relation of cause and effect. Attributing, then, the symbolical character of the rose to its tutelary planet, they regard the earth in the same light as the ancients did the chaste Diana, and believe that she plants this her favourite flower in the moon, whenever she loses a votary. The priesthood encourage this superstition, as they have grafted on it some mystical rites, which add to their power and profit, and which one of our Pundits thinks has a great resemblance to the Eleusinian mysteries. There is, however, my dear Atterley, little satisfaction in tracing the origin of vulgar superstitions. They grow up like a strange plant in a forest, without our being able to tell how the seed found its way there. It is generally believed in the east, that the moon, at particular periods of her revolution round the earth, has a great influence in causing rain; though every one must see, that, notwithstanding such influence must be the same in every part of the earth, it is invariably fair in one place, at the very time that it is rainy in another. Nay, we may safely aver that there is not a day, nor an hour, in the year, in which it is not dry and rainy, cloudy and clear, windy and calm, in hundreds of places at once."

I told the Brahmin that the same opinion prevailed in my country. That the vulgar also believe the moon, according to its age, to have particular effects on the flesh of slaughtered animals; and that all sailors distinguish between a wet and a dry day, according to the position of the crescent.

We then inquired of the warden of this flowery plain, if he had ever remarked any difference in the number of roses which sprung up in a given period of time. He said he thought they were more numerous about five and twenty or thirty years ago, than he had ever seen them before or since. With that exception, he said, the number appeared to be nearly the same every year.

The Brahmin happening to be in one of those pleasant moods which are occasionally experienced by amiable tempers, even when under the pressure of sorrow and age, now amused himself in pointing out the flowers which probably represented the different nations of the earth; and when he saw any one remarkably small, pale and delicate, he insisted that it belonged to his own country; which point, however, I, not yielding to him in nationality, warmly contested. I would here remark, that as the rose is called **gul** in the Persian language and the ancient Sanscrit, the name of this field furnished another argument in support of the Brahmin's hypothesis of the origin of the moon.

While thus oblivious of the past, and reckless of the future, we were enjoying the present moment in this **badinage**, and I was extolling the odour of the rose, as beyond every other grateful to the olfactory nerves of man, a lively, flippant little personage came up, and accosted the Brahmin with the familiarity of an acquaintance. My companion immediately introduced me to him, and at the same time gave me to understand that this was the great Reffei, one of the most distinguished literati of the country. Although his eye was remarkably piercing, I perceived in it somewhat of the wildness which always characterizes a Glonglim. He was evidently impatient for discussion; and having informed himself of the subject of my rhapsody when he joined our party, he vehemently exclaimed,--"I am surprised at your falling in with that popular prejudice; while it is easy to show, that but for some feeling of love, or pity, or admiration, with which the rose happens to be associated--some past pleasure which it brings to your recollection, or some future pleasure which it suggests,--any other flower would be equally sweet. You see the rose a very beautiful flower; and you have been accustomed, whenever you saw and felt its beauty, to perceive, at the same time, a certain odour. The beauty and the odour thus become associated in your mind, and the smell brings along with it the pleasure you feel in looking at it. But the chief part of the gratification you receive from smelling a rose, arises from some past scene of delight of which it reminds you; as, of the days of your innocence and childhood, when you ran about the garden--or when you were decorated with nosegays--or danced round a may-pole, (this is rather a free translation)--or presented a bunch of flowers to some little favourite." He said a great deal more on the subject, and spoke so prettily and ingeniously, as almost to make a convert of me; when, on bringing my nose once more to the flower, I found in it the same exquisite fragrance as ever.

"Why do we like," he continued, "the smell of a beef-steak, or of a cup of tea, except for the pleasure we receive from their taste?"

I mentioned, as an exception to his theory, the codfish, which is esteemed a very savoury dish by my countrymen, but which no one ever regarded as very fragrant. But he repelled my objection by an ingenious hypothesis, grounded on certain physiological facts, to show that this supposed disagreeable smell was also the effect of some early associations. I then mentioned to him assafoetida, the odour of which I believed was universally odious. He immediately replied, that we are always accustomed to associate with this drug, the disagreeable ideas of sickness, female weakness, hysterics, affectation, &c. Unable to continue the argument, I felt myself vanquished. I again stooped to the flower, and as I inhaled its perfume, "Surely," said I to myself, "this rose would be sweet if I were to lose my memory altogether:" but recollecting the great Reffei's argument, I mentally added thanks to divine philosophy, which always corrects our natural prejudices.

CHAPTER XV.

Atterley goes to the great monthly fair--Its various exhibitions; difficulties--Preparations to leave the Moon--Curiosities procured by Atterley--Regress to the Earth.

The philosopher, not waiting to enjoy the triumph of victory, abruptly took his leave, and we, refreshed and delighted with our walk, returned home. Our landlord informed us that we had arrived in good time to attend the great fair, or market, which regularly takes place a little before the sun sinks below the horizon. Having taken a short repast, while the Brahmin called on one of his acquaintance, I sallied forth into the street, and soon found myself in the bustling throng, who were hastening to this great resort of the busy, the idle, the knavish, and the gay; some in pursuit of gain, and some of pleasure; whilst others again, without any settled purpose, were carried along by the vague desire of meeting with somewhat to relieve them from the pain of idleness.

The fair was held in a large square piece of ground in one of the suburbs, set apart for that purpose; and on each of its four sides a long low building, or rather roof, supported on massy white columns, extended about six hundred yards in length, and was thirty yards wide. Immediately within this arcade were arranged the finer kinds of merchandise, fabrics of cotton or silk, and articles of jewelry, cutlery, porcelain, and glass. On the outside were provisions of every kind, vegetable and animal, flesh, fish, and fowl, as well as the coarser manufactures. At no great distance from this hollow square, (which was used exclusively for buying and selling,) might be seen an infinite variety of persons, collected in groupes, all engaged in some occupation or amusement, according to their several tastes and humours. Here a party of young men were jumping, or wrestling, or shooting at a mark with cross-bows. There, girls and boys were dancing to the sound of a pipe, or still smaller children were playing at marbles, or amusing themselves with the toys they had just purchased. Not far from these, a quack from one scaffold was descanting on the virtues of his medicines, whilst a preacher from another was holding forth to the graver part of the crowd, the joys and terrors of another life; and yet farther on, a motley groupe were listening to a blind beggar, who was singing to the music of a sort of rude guitar. Here and there curtains, hanging from a slight frame of wood-work, veiled a small square from the eyes of all, except those who paid a nail for admittance. Some of these curtained boxes contained jugglers--some tumblers--some libidinous pictures--and others again, strange birds, beasts, and other animals. I observed that none of the exhibitions were as much frequented as these booths; and I was told that the corporation of the city derived from them a considerable revenue. Amidst such an infinite variety of objects, my attention was so distracted that it could not settle down upon any one, and I strolled about without object or design.

When I had become more familiar with this mixed multitude of sights and sounds, I endeavoured to take a closer survey of some of the objects composing the medley. The first thing which attracted my particular notice, was a profusion of oaths and imprecations, which proceeded from one of the curtained booths. I paid the admittance money to a well-dressed man, of smooth, easy manners, and entered. I found there several parties paired off, and engaged at different games; but, like the rest of the bystanders, I felt myself most strongly attracted towards the two who were betting highest. One of these was an elderly man, of a tall stature, in a plain dress; the other was a short man, in very costly apparel, and some years younger. For a long time the scales of victory seemed balanced between them; but at length the tall man, who had great self-possession, and who played with consummate skill, won the game: soon after which he rose up, and making a graceful, respectful bow to the rest of the company, he retired. Not being able to catch his eye, so intent was he on his game, I felt some curiosity to know whether he was a Glonglim; but could not ascertain the fact, as some of whom the Brahmin inquired, said that he was, while others maintained that he was not. His adversary, however, evidently belonged to that class, and, when flushed with hope, reminded me of the feather-hunter. At first he endeavoured, by forced smiles, to conceal his rage and disappointment. He then bit his lips with vexation, and challenged one of the bystanders to play for a smaller stake. Fortune seemed about to smile on him on this occasion; but one of the company, who appeared to be very much respected by the rest, detected the little man in some false play, and publicly exposing him, broke up the game. I understood afterwards, that before the fair was over, the gamester avenged himself for this injury in the other's blood: that he then returned to the fair, secretly entered another gambling booth, where he betted so rashly, that he soon lost not only his patrimonial estate, which was large, but his acquired wealth, which was much larger. Having lost all his property, and even his clothes, he then staked and lost his liberty, and even his teeth, which were very good; and he will thus be compelled to live on soups for the rest of his life.

I saw several other matches played, in which great sums were betted, great skill was exhibited, and occasionally much unfairness practised. There was one man in the crowd, whose extraordinary good fortune I could not but admire. He went about from table to table, sometimes betting high and sometimes low, but was generally successful, until he had won as much as he could fairly carry; after which he went out, and amused himself at a puppet-show, and the stall of a cake-woman, with whom he had formerly quarrelled, but who now, when she learnt his success, was obsequiously civil to him. I did not see that he manifested superior skill, but still he was successful; and in his last great stake with a young, but not inexpert player, he won the game, though the chances were three to two against him. "Surely," thought I, "fortune rules the destinies of man in the moon as well as on the earth."

On looking now at my watch, I found that I had been longer a witness of these trials of skill and fortune, than I had been aware; and on leaving the booth, perceived that the sun had sunk behind the western mountains, and that the earth began to beam with her nocturnal splendour. Those who had come from a distance, were already hurrying back with their carts; and here and there light cars, of various forms and colours, and drawn by dogs, were conveying those away whose object had been amusement. Some were snatching a hasty meal; and a few, by their quiet air, seemed as if they meant to continue on the spot as long as the regulations permit, after sunset, which is about twenty of our hours. I found the Brahmin at home when I returned, and I felt as much pleased to see him, as if we had not seen each other for many months.

As the shades of night approached, my anxiety to return to my native planet increased, and I urged my friend to lose no time in preparing for our departure. We were soon afterwards informed that a man high in office, and renowned for his political sagacity, proposed to detain us, on the ground that when such voyages as ours were shown to be practicable, the inhabitants of the earth, who were so much more numerous than those of the moon, might invade the latter with a large army, for the purposes of rapine and conquest. We farther learnt that this opinion, which was at first cautiously circulated in the higher circles, had become more generally known, and was producing a strong sensation among the people.

The Brahmin immediately presented himself before the council of state, to remove the impression. He pointed out to them the insurmountable obstacles to such an invasion, physical and moral. He urged to them that the nations of the earth felt so much jealousy and ill-will towards one another, that they never cordially co-operated in any enterprise for their common interest or glory; and that if any one nation were to send an army into the moon, such a scheme of ambition would afford at once a temptation and pretext for its neighbours to invade it. That his country had not the ability, and mine had not the inclination, to attack the liberties of any other: so far from that, he informed them, on my authority, that we were in the habit of sending teachers abroad, to instruct other nations in the duties of religion, morals, and humanity. He entered into some calculations, to show that the project was also impracticable on account of its expense; and, lastly, insisted that if all other difficulties were removed, we should find it impossible to convince the people of the earth that we had really been to the moon. I have since found that the Brahmin was more right in his last argument, than I then believed possible.

I am not able to say what effect these representations of the Brahmin would have produced, if they had not been taken up and enforced by the political rival of him who had first opposed our departure; but by his powerful aid they finally triumphed, and we obtained a formal permission to leave the moon whenever, we thought proper.

As we meant to return in the same machine in which we came, we were not long in preparing for our voyage. We proposed to set out about the middle of the night; and we passed the chief part of the interval in making visits of ceremony, and in calling on those who had shown us civility. I endeavoured also, to collect such articles as I thought would be most curious and rare in my own country, and most likely to produce conviction with those who might be disposed to question the fact of my voyage. I was obliged, however, to limit myself to such things as were neither bulky nor weighty, the Brahmin thinking that after we had taken in our instruments and the necessary provisions, we could not safely take more than twenty or thirty pounds in addition.

Some of my lunar curiosities, which I thought would be most new and interesting to my countrymen, have proved to be very familiar to our men of science. This has been most remarkably the case with my mineral specimens. Of the leaves and flowers of above seventy plants, which I brought, more than forty are found on the earth, and several of these grow in my native State. With the insects I have been more successful; but some of these, as well as of the plants, I am assured, are found on the coasts of the Pacific, or in the islands of that ocean; which fact, by the way, gives a farther support to the Brahmin's hypothesis.

Besides the productions of nature that I have mentioned, I procured some specimens of their cloth, a few light toys, a lady's turban decorated with cantharides, a pair of slippers with heavy metallic soles, which are used there for walking in a strong wind, and by the dancing girls to prevent their jumping too high. As this metal, which gravitates to the moon, is repelled from the earth, these slippers assist the wearer here in springing from the ground as much as they impeded it in the moon, and therefore I have lent them to Madame ----, of the New-York Theatre, who is thus enabled to astonish and delight the spectators with her wonderful lightness and agility.

But there is nothing that I have brought which I prize so highly as a few of their manuscripts. The Lunarians write as we do, from left to right; but when their words consist of more than one syllable, all the subsequent syllables are put over the first, so that what we call ***long words***, they call ***high*** ones: which mode of writing makes them more striking to the eye. This peculiarity has, perhaps, had some effect in giving their writers a magniloquence of style, something like that which so laudably characterises our Fourth of July Orations and Funeral Panegyrics: that composition being thought the finest in which the words stand highest. Another advantage of this mode of writing is, that they can crowd more in a small page, so that a long discourse, if it is also very eloquent, may be compressed in a single page. I have left some of the manuscripts with the publisher of this work, for the gratification of the public curiosity.

Having taken either respectful or affectionate leave of all, and got every thing in readiness, on the 20th day of August, 1825, about midnight we again entered our copper balloon, if I may so speak, and rose from the moon with the same velocity as we had formerly ascended from the earth. Though I experienced somewhat of my former sensations, when I again found myself off the solid ground, yet I soon regained my self-possession; and, animated with the hope of seeing my children and country, with the past success of our voyage, and (I will not disguise it,) with the distinction which I expected it would procure me from my countrymen, I was in excellent spirits. The Brahmin exhibited the same mild equanimity as ever.

As the course of our ascent was now less inclined from the vertical line than before, in proportion as the motion of the moon on its axis, is slower than that of the earth, we for some hours could see the former, only by the light reflected from our planet; and although the objects on the moon's surface were less distinct, they appeared yet more beautiful in my eyes than they had done in the glare of day. The difference, however, may be in part attributed to my being now in a better frame of mind for enjoying the scene. As our distance increased, the face of the moon became of a lighter and more uniform tint, until at length it looked like one vast lake of melted silver, with here and there small pieces of greyish dross floating on it. After contemplating this lovely and magnificent spectacle for about an hour, I turned to the Brahmin, and reminded him of his former promise to give me the history of his early life. He replied, "as you have seen all that you can see of the moon, and the objects of the earth are yet too indistinct to excite much interest, I am not likely to have a more suitable occasion;" and after a short pause, he began in the way that the reader may see in the next chapter.

CHAPTER XVI.

The Brahmin gives Atterley a history of his life.

I have already informed you that I was born at Benares, which, as you know, is a populous city on the banks of the Ganges, and the most celebrated seat of Hindoo science and literature. My father was a priest of Vishun, of a high rank; and as his functions required him to live within the precincts of the Pagoda, he was liberally maintained out of its ample revenues. I was his only son, and according to the usage of our country, was destined to the same holy calling. At an early age I was put under a private tutor, and then sent to one of the schools attached to the Pagoda. Upon what little matters, my dear Atterley, do our fortunes, and even our characters depend! Had I been sent to another school, the whole destiny of my life would have been changed.

"I was in my twelfth year when I entered this school, which contained from thirty to forty boys about my age. The cleverest of these was Balty Mahu, who, like myself, belonged to the higher order of Brahmins. He took the lead, not only in the exercises within the school, but in all the sports and pastimes out of it. Nature, however, had not been equally kind to him in temper and disposition. He was restless, ambitious, proud, vindictive, and implacable. He could occasionally, too, practise cunning and deception; although anger and violence were more congenial to his nature.

"It soon appeared that I was to be his rival in the school, and from that moment he cordially hated me. The praises that had previously been lavished on him by the teacher, were now shared by me, and most of the boys secretly rejoiced to see his proud spirit humbled. In our sports I was also his successful competitor. Nature had given me an excellent constitution; and though I had not a very robust frame,

I could boast of great agility and flexibility of limbs. When the sun had descended behind the mountain which screened our play-ground from his evening rays, we commonly amused ourselves in foot-races, and other pastimes, of which running was an important part. In this exercise I had no equal. I could also jump higher and farther than any boy in school, except one, and that one was not Balty Mahu.

"His ill-will was not slow in manifesting itself. He took every occasion of contradicting me: sometimes indulged in sly sneers at my expense, and now and then even attempted to turn me into open ridicule. I always replied with spirit; but I found such contests as disagreeable to me as they were new. One evening, under the pretext that I had purposely jostled him in running, he struck me, and we fought. Although he was probably stronger than I, as he was heavier and older, my suppleness enabled me to get the better of him in a wrestle; and I got him under me, when the master, attracted by the shouts of the boys, made his appearance. He separated and reproved us, and sent us off in disgrace to our respective rooms. From that time Balty Mahu treated me with more outward respect than before; but I believe he hated me with more rancour than ever.

"I had now become the general favourite of the boys. The school was, indeed, divided into parties, but mine was much the strongest; and of those who adhered to my rival, very few seemed cordially to dislike me. Though this state of things was very annoying to me, it proved advantageous in one respect, as it made me more diligent in my studies, lest I should furnish my rival with an occasion of triumphing ever me; so that I owe a part of what I gained to the enmity of my rival.

"When I had reached my sixteenth year, I was removed to the college in Benares. This is commonly a very interesting event in the life of a youth, as it reminds him that he is drawing near the period of manhood, and leaves him more a master of his actions. But on the present occasion my pleasure had two drawbacks: I could not but feel the contrast between the warm and confiding attachment of my late school-fellows, and the coldness and reserve of my new companions. Yet the most disagreeable circumstance was, that I here met with my former rival, Balty Mahu. He had entered the college about a month before me, and, aware of my intention, had spared no pains, as I afterwards learnt, of prejudicing the students against me.

"After a few months, however, our relative standing was the same here as it had been at the school. I gradually overcame the prejudices of the students, and gained their good will, while he was always giving offence by his meddlesome disposition and overbearing manners: yet his talents and force of character always procured him a few followers, whom he managed as he pleased. Of their aid he made use to gratify his malevolence towards me, for this feeling had grown with his growth, and now seemed to be the master passion of his breast. I was able to trace the result of their machinations every where. Sometimes it was intimated to the teachers that I had been assisted in my exercises; at others, that I had infringed the college rules, or had put false reports in circulation, or had neglected some of the many ceremonies required by our religion. This was their favourite, as well as the most efficient mode of attack, as in these respects there was some colour for their accusation.

"In my early childhood I had been spared, by the tenderest of mothers, from many of the ablutions practised by the Hindoos, under the belief that they would be injurious to my constitution, which, though healthy, had never been robust. A foundation was thus laid with me for habitual remissness in these ceremonies; and after I grew up, I persuaded myself that they were of less importance than they were deemed by my countrymen. My chief delight had ever been in books; and although, when engaged in active pursuits, I took a lively interest in them for the time, I always returned to my first love with unabated ardour.

"Some of these accusations, being utterly groundless, I was able to disprove; but the few that were true I endeavoured to excuse, and thus, by their admission, credit was procured for their most unfounded calumny. These petty transgressions, (for I cannot even now regard them as sins,) industriously reported and artfully exaggerated, did me lasting injury with all the most pious of our caste. The charitable portion, indeed, were merely estranged from me; but the more bigoted part began to regard me with aversion and horror.

"In one of our vacations, my father allowed me to visit a brother of his, who lived in the country, about thirty miles from Benares. My uncle had two sons, of nearly my own age, and several daughters. With the former I rode, played chess, and engaged in such sports as are not forbidden to my profession; but my female cousins I seldom saw, as they rarely left their Zenana, into which I was not permitted to enter. I was of an age to be desirous of becoming better acquainted with my female cousins, especially after I learnt that they then had as guests, a lady and her daughter, who had come to pass some weeks here during the absence of her husband, then employed in some public mission to Calcutta. But it was only now and then that I had been able to catch a transient and distant view of these females, during the first week after my arrival; and the little I saw, served but to increase my curiosity. Chance, however, soon afforded me the means of gratifying it.

"An important festival in our calendar was now approaching, and preparations were made to celebrate it in various modes, and, amongst others, by a fight between a *royal* tiger and an elephant. For several days all was bustle and confusion in my uncle's family. Howdahs, newly gilded and painted, were provided for the elephants--new caparisons for the horses--new liveries for the attendants--cloth and silk, of the richest dyes and hues, united with a profusion of gold and silver ornaments, to dazzle the eye with their varied splendour. This was one of those exhibitions, which those who were intended for the priesthood, were prohibited from attending. I confess, when I witnessed these showy and costly preparations, and pictured to myself the magnificent scene for which they were intended--those formidable animals contending in mortal conflict--the thousands of gaily dressed spectators, gazing in breathless anxiety,--I repined at my lot, and regretted I had not been born in a condition which, though of less dignity, would not have cut me off from some of the most exquisite pleasures of life. At length the important day arrived, and I found my mortification so acute, that I determined to withdraw myself, as much as I could, from a scene that I could not witness without pain. Among my acquirements at college, was a knowledge of your language; and I had now begun to take the liveliest interest in its beautiful fictions, which I greatly preferred to ours, as being more true to nature, and as exhibiting women in characters at once lovely, pure, and elevated. I was then reading "The Vicar of Wakefield," and had reached the middle of that interesting tale, on the morning of the festival, when my tranquillity was interrupted in the way I have mentioned. Accordingly, taking my book and English dictionary, I retired to a small summer-house at the foot of the garden, and determined to remain there till the cavalcade had set out. It was some time before I could fix my attention on what I read; but after a while, the interest the book had previously excited returned, and I became at length so engrossed by the incidents of the story, as to forget the festival, the procession, the tiger, and the elephant, as much as if they had never before entered my head.

"After some hours passed in this intellectual banquet, I waked from my day dream, and I thought again of the spectacle with a feeling bordering on indifference. I walked towards the house, where all appeared to be still and silent as a desert. I entered it, and of the forty or fifty menials belonging to it, not one was to be seen. Those who were not in attendance on the family, had sought some respite from their ordinary labours. The Zenana then caught my eye, and I felt irresistibly impelled to enter it. I used great caution, however, looking around me in every direction as I proceeded there. I found the same silence and desertion as in the other parts of the mansion. I passed through a sitting-room into a long gallery, with which the bed-chambers of the ladies communicated. The doors were all open, and the whole interior of their apartments exhibited so strange a medley of unseemly objects, and such utter disorder, as materially to affect my opinion of female delicacy, and to damp my desire of becoming acquainted with my cousins. I passed on, with a feeling of disappointment bordering on disgust, when I came to a room which went far to redeem the character of the sex in my estimation. Here all was neatness and propriety: every thing was either in place, or only enough out of it to indicate the recent occupation of the room, or to show the taste or talent of the occupant; such as a book left half open at one end of an ottoman, and a piece of embroidery at the other. The flowers too, which decorated the room, showed by their freshness that they had not long left their beds. I could not help stopping to survey a scene which accorded so well with my previous notions of female refinement. At the end of the gallery was a veranda, facing the east, and surrounded by lattices. In this were a number of flower-pots, arranged with the same air of neatness and taste as had been conspicuous in the chamber. I entered it, for the purpose of looking into the flower-garden, with which it communicated; and on approaching the lattice, I saw, seated in an alcove not far from the veranda, a face and form that struck me as being the most beautiful I had ever beheld. I remained for some time riveted to the spot, but soon found myself irresistibly impelled to get a nearer view of the lovely object. With as light a step and as little noise as possible, I descended into the garden from the veranda, and approaching the alcove on the side where its foliage was thickest, I found that the beauty, of which I had before thought so highly, did not appear less on a closer survey. The vision on which I gazed in silent rapture, a maiden, who, though she had apparently attained her full stature, did not seem to be more than thirteen or fourteen years of age. Her eyes had the brightness and fulness of the antelope's, but, owing to their long silken lashes, were yet more expressive of softness than of spirit; and at this time they evinced more than usual languor. She was in a rich undress, and was apparently an invalid. Her long raven locks hung with careless grace, partly behind, and partly over, a neck that might have served as a model for the sculptor. She was looking wistfully on a bunch of flowers in her hand, which I felt pleasure in recognising to be the same I had seen on the piece of embroidery. I feared to advance, lest I should give offence; but I felt also unable to retreat. I fancied I saw one of those lovely and dignified females which the writers in your language describe so well. But a sudden movement of the fair damsel to get up, bringing me full in her view, she started back with alarm and surprise, and in a moment afterwards her cheek, which had been before pale, almost to European whiteness, was deeply suffused. I respectfully approached her, and inquired if she was one of my cousins. She answered in the negative; said she was on a visit to the family, to whom she was related: added that she had not expected to see any one in the garden; but this was said as if she meant rather to apologise for her undress, than to reproach me for my intrusion. These remarks were uttered with a propriety and sweetness that won upon me yet more than her beauty. I then, in return, assured her that I had not supposed any of the family had remained at home, when I strolled to this part of the mansion. I begged she would not regard me with the formality of a stranger; and insisted that, as she was the cousin of my relation, she was also mine. To this ingenious argument she answered with so much good sense, and at the same time, so much gentleness and artlessness, that I thought I could have listened to her for ever. While I spoke, she continued to move on. I entreated to know if she was satisfied with my apology; repeated that I had not meant to intrude on her privacy. She mildly replied that she was. I then asked permission to call her cousin. She said she should not object, if it would gave me pleasure. It was, my dear Atterley, her ineffable sweetness of disposition, and of manners so entirely free from pride, coquetry, or affectation, in which this lovely creature excelled all other women, yet more than in beauty and grace. I then inquired when I should again see my lovely cousin. She replied, "I walk in the great garden sometimes with my companions, when their brothers are away; but the girls will not think it proper to walk when you are there." Perceiving that I looked chagrined, she added: "It is said, you know, that the light from mens' eyes is yet worse for womens' faces than the light of the sun;" and she blushed as if she had said something wrong. I stammered out I know not what extravagant compliment in reply, and entreated that I might have an opportunity of seeing and conversing with her sometimes: to which she promptly answered that she should not object, if her mother approved it. I inquired why she had not attended the exhibition; when I learnt from her, that, as she had been slightly indisposed the day before, and her mother being unwilling she should expose herself to the heat of the weather and the crowd, she had been left under the care of her nurse; but that finding herself better, she had permitted her attendants to walk over the grounds, while she amused herself in embroidery; and that she had come into the garden to get a fresh supply of the flowers she was working.

"She had by this time approached a small gate, which communicated with the apartments on the ground-floor of the Zenana; when, turning to me, she said, "You can return the way you came, but I must leave you here;" and, making a slight bow, she sprung like a young fawn through the gate, and was out of sight in a moment.

"You may wonder, my dear Atterley, that I should remember all these minute circumstances, after the lapse of more than forty years; but every incident of that day is as fresh in my memory as the occurrence of yesterday. To this single green spot in my existence, my mind is never tired of returning.

"I continued for some time in a sort of dreaming ecstasy; but as soon as I collected my thoughts, I began to devise some scheme by which I could again have the happiness of seeing and conversing with the lovely Veenah. My brain had before that time teemed with ambitious projects of distinguishing myself; sometimes as a priest--sometimes as a writer; and occasionally I thought I would bend all my efforts to rouse my countrymen to throw off the ignominious yoke of Great Britain. But this short interview had changed the whole current of my thoughts. I had now a new set of feelings, opinions, and wishes. My mind dwelt solely upon the pleasures of domestic life--the surpassing bliss of loving and of being beloved.

"When the cavalcade returned in the evening, its gaudy magnificence, which I would not permit myself even to see in the morning, I now regarded with cold indifference; nay, more, I congratulated myself on having missed the exhibition, though a few hours before I had deemed this privation one of the misfortunes of my life.

"The next day I went to the garden betimes; and as it communicated with the shrubbery and grounds attached to the Zenana, and the males of the family occasionally entered it when the ladies were not present, I prevailed on the gardener to grant me admission, under the pretext of gathering some uncommonly fine mangoes, which were then ripe. I went to the several spots where I had first seen Veenah--where I had conversed with her--where I had parted from her; and they each had some secret and indescribable charm for me. I fear, Atterley, I fatigue you. The feelings of which I speak, are fully known only to the natives of warm climates, and to those but once in their lives."

I assured him that he was mistaken; that the emotions he described, were the same in all countries, and at all times, and begged him to proceed.

"I repeated my visit," he continued, "several times the same day, under any pretext I could invent--to gather an orange, or other fruit--to pluck a rose--to frighten away mischievous birds--to catch the unobstructed breeze, or sit in a cooler shade; in which artifices I played a part that had before been foreign to my nature. I was disappointed, however, in my wishes. I thought, indeed, I once saw some one in the veranda, looking through the lattice into the garden, but the figure soon disappeared.

"On the following day I had the satisfaction to hear my young companions propose to go on a fishing party, an amusement in which, by the rules of my caste, I was not allowed to partake. They had scarcely left the house before I flew to the garden with a book in my hand, and passing as before to the shrubbery, I buried myself in a close thicket at one end of it. I remained there from the morning till late in the afternoon, without refreshment of any kind; and such was the intensity of my emotion, that I did not feel the want of it. At length, a little before sunset, I saw Veenah and her three cousins enter the garden. I soon contrived to show myself, with my book in my hand. I approached, bowed to them all, but to Veenah last; and although my cousins showed surprise at seeing me in their garden, at this time, they did not seem displeased. I felt very desirous, I could not tell why, to conceal my feelings from every person except her who was the object of them. I forced a conversation with my two eldest cousins, who were modest pleasing girls, and then with an embarrassed air addressed a few words to Veenah and her companion, the youngest of my cousins. Occasionally I would stray off from them as if I was about to leave them, and then suddenly return. In one of these movements, I perceived that Veenah and her associate had separated from the others, and strolled to a distant part of the garden. I soon joined them as if it were by accident, entered into conversation with them alternately, and of course only one half of that which I either heard or said proceeded from the heart or found its way thither. I know not if Veenah expected to see me, but she was dressed with unusual care. We had not been conversing many minutes before the eldest sister beckoning to them, they bid me good night and returned to the house.

"To the same sort of management I had recourse every day, and seldom failed to see and converse with Veenah, sometimes in company with all her cousins, but oftener with Fatima, the youngest. By dividing my attentions among them all, I succeeded for a while in concealing from them the object of my preference; but the sex are too sharp-sighted to be long deceived in these matters. As soon as I perceived that my secret was discovered, I endeavoured to make a friend of Fatima, in which I was successful. After this our meetings were more frequent, and what was of greater importance, they were uninterrupted. Fatima, who was one of the most generous and amiable girls in the world, would often take Veenah out to walk, when her sisters were otherwise engaged; at which times she was perpetually contriving, under some little pretext, to leave us alone. We were not long in understanding each other; and when I urged our early marriage, she ingenuously replied, that I had her consent whenever I had her father's, and that she hoped I could obtain that; but added, (and she trembled while she spoke) she did not know his views respecting her. In the first raptures of requited affection, what lover thinks of difficulties? In obtaining Veenah's heart I believed that all mine were at an end, and my time was passed in one dream of unmixed delight. Oh! what happiness I enjoyed in these interviews--in seeing Veenah--in gazing on her lovely features--in listening to her sentiments, that were sometimes gay and thoughtless, sometimes serious and melancholy, but always tender and affectionate,--and now and then, when not perceived, in venturing to take her hand. These fleeting joys are ever recurring to my imagination, to show me what my lot might have been, and to contrast it with its sad reverse!

"The time now approached for Veenah and her mother to return to Benares. On the evening before they set out, Fatima contrived for us a longer interview than usual. It was as melancholy as it was tender. But in the midst of my grief, at the prospect of our separation, I recollected that we were soon to meet again in the city; while Veenah's tears, for she did not attempt to disguise or suppress her feelings, seemed already to forebode that our happiness was here to terminate.

"When about to part, we exchanged amaranths I took her hand to bid her adieu, and, without seeming to intend it, our lips met, and the first kiss of love was moistened with a tear. Pardon me, Atterley, nature will have her way."--And here the venerable man wept aloud.

I availed myself of this interruption to the narrative, to propose to my venerable friend to take some refreshment. Having partaken of a frugal repast, and invigorated ourselves, each with about four hours sleep, the Brahmin thus resumed his story.

CHAPTER XVII.

The Brahmin's story continued--The voyage concluded--Atterley and the Brahmin separate--Atterley arrives in New--York.

I was not slow to follow Veenah to the city, and as had been agreed upon, had to ask the consent of her father to our union, as soon as I had obtained the approbation of my own. Here I met with a difficulty which I had not expected. My partial father had formed very high hopes of my future advancement, and thought that an early marriage, though not incompatible with my profession, or a successful discharge of its duties, would put an end to my ambition, or at all events, lessen my exertions. He first urged me to postpone my wishes, till I had completed my college course, and had by travelling seen something of the world. But finding me immoveable on this point, he then suggested that I might meet with serious obstacles from Veenah's father, whom he represented as remarkable both for his avarice and his bigotry; that consequently he was likely to dispose of his daughter to the son-in-law who could pay most liberally for her; and that the imputations which had been cast on my religious creed, would reach his ears, if they had not already done so, and be sure to prejudice him against me.

"These last considerations prevailed on me to defer my application to Shunah Shoo, until the suspicions regarding my faith had either died away, or been falsified by my scrupulous observance of all religious duties. My excellent mother, who at first had entered into my feelings and seconded my views, readily acquiesced in the good sense of my father's advice.

"My next object was to communicate this to Veenah. I accordingly sat down, and wrote a full account of all that had occurred, and folding up the packet, hurried to the opposite quarter of the town where Shunah Shoo lived. It was then in the dusk of the evening, and I was fearful it was too late for me to be recognised; but after I had taken two or three turns in the street, I saw the white amaranth I had given Veenah, suspended by a thread from the lattice of an upper window. I immediately held up the packet, and soon afterwards a cord was let down from the same lattice to the ground. To this I hastily fastened the paper, and passed on to avoid observation. The next evening you may be sure I was at the same spot. The little amaranth again announced that I was recognised; and as soon as we were satisfied that no one was observing us, the cord let down one letter and took up another. Veenah's pen had given an expression to her feelings, that her tongue had never ventured to do before. She moreover commended my course--besought me to be prudent--and above all, to do nothing to offend her father.

"The first letter which a lover receives from his mistress, is a new era in his life. Again and again I kissed the precious paper, and almost wore it out in my bosom. We afterwards improved in this mode of intercourse, and, by various preconcerted signals, were able to carry on our correspondence altogether in the night. Not a day passed that we did not exchange letters, which, though they contained few facts, and always expressed the same sentiments, still repeated what we were never tired of hearing. To the moment at which I was to receive a letter from Veenah, my thoughts were continually and anxiously turned: and it now seems to me as if our passion was inflamed yet more by this sort of intercourse, than by our personal interviews. I am convinced it wrought more powerfully upon our imaginations. In the mean time I continued my daily attendance at college, though my studies were utterly neglected, one single object absorbing all my thoughts and feelings.

"I know not whether the evident change in my habits induced my old enemy, Balty Mahu, to observe my motions. But so it was, that one moonlight night I thought I was watched by some person; and on the following night an individual of the same figure, and whom I now suspected to be Balty Mahu, came suddenly from a cross street, and passed near me. A few evenings afterwards, instead of a letter, I received a scrap of paper from Veenah, on which was written the following words:--

"We are discovered. Balty Mahu, who is my relative and your enemy, has been here. He has persuaded my father that you are an unbeliever. I am denied pen and ink. If you cannot convince my father of his error, O! pity, and try to forget, your unhappy VEENAH."

"This writing was indistinctly traced with a burnt stick, on a blank leaf torn out of a book. In the first moment of indignation, I felt disposed to seek Balty Mahu, the great enemy of my life, and wreak my vengeance on him for all his persecutions; but the conviction that such a course would extinguish the last spark of hope, restrained me. I then determined to see Shunah Shoo, and endeavour to remove his prejudices. I accordingly called on him at his own house: but after he had heard my vindication, (to which he evidently gave no credit,) he coolly told me that he meant to dispose of his daughter in another way. The words fell like ice upon my heart. I expostulated; and, offensive as was his haughty air, even had recourse to entreaty. But he, in a yet harsher manner, told me that he must be permitted to manage his own affairs in his own way; and added, that he did not wish to be longer prevented from attending to them. I was compelled to retire, with my heart almost as full of hatred for the father, as of love for the child.

"On the same night, I again betook myself to the street in which Shunah Shoo lived, but not by the ordinary route. I cautiously approached his house. All was stillness and quiet: no light appeared to be burning in Veenah's room, nor indeed in any other part of the house. I hence concluded that they had now deprived her of light, as well as of pen and ink. I continued in the street until near morning, straining my eyes and ears in the hope of catching something that would give me intelligence concerning her. Often, in the course of that painful suspense, did I fancy I heard a noise at the lattice in Veenah's apartment, or in some other part of the mansion; and once I persuaded myself I saw a light: but these illusions served only to aggravate my disappointment. The next morning, before I had left my room, my father informed me that Shunah Shoo, with his family, had left Benares early the preceding evening; but whither they had gone, he had not learnt.

"I rose, and immediately set about discovering their course; but all I could learn was, that they had embarked in one of the passage-boats which ply on the Ganges, and that Shunah had taken his palanquins and many of his servants with him: and, as Balty Mahu had suddenly absented himself from college at the same time, I did not doubt that he had aided in executing the plan which he had also probably formed. My father, who saw what I suffered, spared no pains to discover the place of their retreat; but our endeavours were all ineffectual.

"At the end of three months, in which time my anxiety increased rather than diminished, the mystery was dispelled. It was now trumpeted through the city, that Shunah Shoo had returned to Benares in great pomp, accompanied by a wealthy Omrah of a neighbouring district, to whom he had given, or rather sold, his daughter. The news came upon me like a clap of thunder. My previous state of suspense was happiness compared with what I now felt, when I knew she was in the arms of another. In the first transports of my grief and rage, I could have freely put to death the father, daughter, husband, and myself. I was particularly desirous of seeing Veenah, and venting on her the bitterest reproaches. Unjust that I was! Her sufferings were not inferior to mine; but she had not, like me, the privilege of making them known. I soon found that Hircarrahs, in the pay of Balty Mahu, watched all my motions; and if I had attempted any scheme of vengeance, its execution would have been impracticable.

"After my first transports had subsided into deep and settled grief, my love and tenderness for Veenah returned in full force. I endeavoured to get a sight of her, and thought I should be comparatively happy if I could converse with her, as formerly, though she was the wife of another. After a short time, my uncle's family came to Benares, on a visit to my father and to Shunah Shoo. By the aid of my indulgent mother, who was seriously alarmed for what she saw I suffered, I was able to see Fatima, and to make her the bearer of a letter to Veenah, complaining of her breach of faith, and soliciting an interview. She verbally replied to it through Fatima; and stated, in her justification, that she was hurried from Benares to a town on the river, whence she was rapidly transported to the castle of Omrah, who had not long before lost his wife, and who was more than four times her age. That notwithstanding the notions of filial obedience in which she had been brought up, and the severity with which her father had ever exercised his authority, she had resisted his commands on this occasion, and would have preferred death to marrying the Omrah--nay, would have inflicted it on herself; but that finding her unyielding after all their exertions, they had effected their purpose by a deception which they had practised on her, wherein it seemed that I had unconsciously concurred; for, by means of an intercepted letter of mine to Fatima, in which, hopeless of learning the place of Veenah's retreat, I had expressed an intention of visiting England; and, by the farther aid of some dexterous forgeries, calculated to impose on more experienced minds than hers, they succeeded in persuading her that I had actually set out for Europe, with an intention of never returning. That entertaining no doubt of this intelligence --hopeless of ever seeing me again, and indifferent to every thing besides, she had been led an unresisting victim to the altar.

"Such was the vindication which she considered it just to make me. But all the entreaties of Fatima--all my letters, impassioned as they were, appealing at once to her generosity, humanity, and love,--could not prevail on her to grant me an interview.

"'Tell him,' said she, 'that heaven has forbid it, and to its decrees we are bound to submit. I am now the wife of another, and it is our duty to forget all that is past. But if this be possible, my heart tells me it can be only by our never meeting!'

"In saying this, she wept bitterly; but at the same time exacted a promise from Fatima, that she would never mention the subject to her again. Finding her thus inexorable, I fell into a settled melancholy, and my health was visibly declining. The Europeans consider the natives of Hindostan to be feeble and effeminate; but the soul, that which distinguishes man from brutes, acts with an intensity and constancy of purpose of which they can furnish no examples.

"How long I could have withstood the corrosive effects of my hopeless passion, irritated as it was by my being in the vicinity of its object--by hearing perpetually of her beauty, and sometimes catching a glimpse of it,--I know not; but the Omrah, after a few months spent with his father-in-law, returned with his bride to his castle in the country. Yielding now to the wishes of my anxious parents, I consented to travel. I was at first benefited by the exercise and change of scene; but after a while, my melancholy returned, and my health grew worse. Though indifferent to life itself, and all that it now promised, I exerted myself for the sake of my parents, especially of my mother, who suffered so acutely on my account: but I carried a barbed arrow in my heart, and the greater the efforts to extract it, the more they rankled the wound.

"After spending more than a year in travelling, first through the mountainous district of our country, and then along the coast, and finding no change for the better, I determined to try the effect of a sea voyage. I accordingly embarked at Calcutta, in a coasting vessel that was bound to Madras. At this time I had wasted away to a mere skeleton, and no one who saw me, believed I could live a month.

Such, indeed, were my own impressions. In the letter which I wrote to my parents, I endeavoured to prepare them for the worst. When, after a long voyage, we reached Madras, my health was evidently improved; but a piece of intelligence I here received, had perhaps a still greater effect I learnt that Balty Mahu, who had kept himself concealed from me before I left Benares, had lately visited Madras, on a travelling tour. This news operated on me like a charm. The idea of avenging myself on the author of all my calamities, infused new life into my exhausted frame, and from the moment that I determined to pursue him, I felt like another man.

"You must not, however, suppose that I even then entertained the purpose of taking away my enemy's life. No, I could not bring my mind exactly to that; but I had a vague, undefined hope, that if we met, some new provocation on his part would afford me just occasion for avenging myself on all; so ingenious, my dear friend, is the sophistry of the passions.

"I lost no time in setting out on the track of Balty Mahu, and, ere many days, overtook him at a small town which he had left just as I entered it, but not before he had received, through his servant, notice of my arrival. My wary enemy, who had little expected to see me here, and who had travelled as much to keep out of my way as to see the country, conjectured my purpose, from the consciousness of what he had done to provoke it. Thus, while we both appeared to others to be merely making a tour of Hindostan, it was soon known to both of us, that my chief purpose was to pursue him, and his to elude my pursuit. In the ardour, as well as exercise of the chase, my health mended rapidly, but I was no nearer the object of my pursuit; for, although I travelled somewhat faster than Bally Mahu, as he wished to avoid the appearance of flying from me, he sometimes contrived to put me on a wrong track. In this way I was once led to travel towards the coast, while he proceeded in an opposite direction to Benares, where he considered he would be most safe from my vengeance, and where the restraints both of religion and law would be more likely to operate on me than in a foreign district.

"My usual practice, on arriving at any town, was to endeavour to learn if Balty Mahu had passed through it; if so, when and in what direction; and to get the information, if possible, without seeming to seek it. On one of these occasions, I heard from a party of merchants that the Omrah Addaway, whose health had been declining for some time, had gone to Benares, for the benefit of medical advice; that his disease, however, had become more serious; and that it was generally thought it would soon occasion his death. What a train of new thoughts, hopes, and desires, did this intelligence excite in me! At first, influenced by the custom of my country, which prohibits widows from marrying again, I thought only of the pleasure of Veenah's society, which I should, of course, be permitted to enjoy, when duty no longer forbade it; but my imagination kindling in its course, I soon pictured her to myself as my wife. The usages which stood in the way of our union, appeared to me barbarous and absurd, and I thought that, banishment from my country, with Veenah, would be infinitely better than any other condition of life without her. These new-born visions so entirely absorbed me, that Balty Mahu was entirely forgotten, or remembered only as we think of an insect which had stung us an hour before. I travelled on at a yet more rapid rate than I had done; and, without stopping on the road to make inquiries, I heard enough to satisfy me that the Omrah could not long survive. When within something more than ten leagues of Benares, I called, about twilight, at a small inn, and meant, after refreshing myself with a few hours' rest, to proceed on my journey. Two travellers were there, who had just left Benares, and had taken up their quarters for the night. They soon fell into conversation about the place they had left, when the mention of Shunah Shoo's name excited my attention.

"'What a shame,' said one, 'that he should have sacrificed that beautiful young creature to the rich old Omrah, when she had so good an offer as Gurameer, the Brahmin Gafawad's only son.'

"'And is it not strange,' said the other, 'that a woman so young and beautiful, should be content to follow to the grave one who is old enough to be her grandfather, and whom she once loathed? But I suppose that that old miser, Shunah Shoo, is at the bottom of it; and, as he deprived her of the man she loved, he has compelled her to sacrifice herself to the one she hates, that he may have her jewels and wealth.'

"'For that matter,' said the first, 'though Shunah Shoo is bad enough for any thing where money is in the way, yet it is said that Veenah goes to the funeral pile of her own accord. She has never seemed to set any value on life since her marriage; and after she heard of Gurameer's death, she has never been seen to smile. Poor young man!'--And here they launched out into a strain of panegyric, which is often bestowed on the dead; but I heeded only the first part of their discourse. Had it not been nearly dark, they must have discovered the force of the feelings which then agitated me. I trembled from head to foot, and, though burning with impatience to obtain from them farther particulars, it was some moments before I could trust myself to speak. At length I asked them when the Suttee would take place; and was answered by one of them, that it would certainly be performed on the following day; and that he had seen the funeral pile himself. Without any farther delay, I set out immediately for the city, and reached it in as short a time as a jaded horse could carry me.

"I came in sight of Benares the next morning, from a hill which overlooks it from the east. The sun was just rising, and pouring a flood of light ever the city, the river, and the surrounding country. Never was contrast greater than between my present feelings, and those which the same spectacle had formerly excited. I now sickened at the prospect, which once would have set my heart bounding with joy. I pressed on in desperate haste, scarcely, however, knowing what I did, being at once overpowered with fatigue, loss of sleep, and harassing emotions. I still had to travel a circuitous course of some two or three miles; and when I reached the city, its crowded population was already in motion: a great multitude of women, of the lower order, with alarm and expectation strongly depicted in their faces, were to be seen mingling in the crowd, and pressing on in the same direction. I would have proceeded immediately to my father's house, but for the fear of being too late. Alighting, therefore, from my horse, I gave him in charge to my servant, whom I sent to inform my parents of my arrival, and to request my father to meet me at the Suttee. I then joined the mixed multitude, which now thronged the streets. Occupied, as my thoughts were, with the scene I was about to witness, and with fears for its issue, they were often interrupted with remarks made in the crowd, in which Veenah's name or mine were mentioned--some lamenting her cruel fate, others pitying mine; but all condemning and execrating Shunah Shoo. Fortunately I was not recognised by any whom I saw. When we reached the spot selected for the sacrifice, the crowd that had there assembled, was not so great as to prevent our getting near the funeral pile; but the numbers continued to augment, until nothing could be seen from the slight eminence on which I stood, but one dense mass of heads, all looking one way, and expressing the intense interest they felt. At length a murmur, like that of distant thunder, ran through the crowd: a passage was, with some difficulty, effected through the multitude by the officers in attendance, and the wretched Veenah made her appearance, supported by her own father on one side, and an uncle on the other--pale enough to be taken for an European--emaciated indeed, but still retaining the same exquisite beauty of features and symmetry of form. She moved with the air of one who was utterly indifferent to the concerns of this world, and to the awful fate which awaited her. She turned her head on hearing the sound of my voice, and, seeing me, shrieked out, "He lives! he lives!" but immediately afterwards fainted in the arms of her supporters: at the same moment I was forcibly held back by some of the attendants, and a number of the bystanders rushed in between us, and intercepted my view. I heard my name now repeated in every direction by the multitude--some calling out to the priests to desist, and others to proceed. I struggled to extricate myself, and passion lent me momentary strength; but it was insufficient. After a short interval, I distinctly heard Veenah imploring them to spare her. I called to the Brahmins who held her, to leave her to herself. I endeavoured to rouse the multitude; but they took the precaution to drown our voices, by the musical instruments which are used on these occasions. Four of these monsters I saw profaning the name of religion, by forcibly placing their victim on the pile, under the show of assisting her to mount it; and there held her down, beside the dead body of her husband, until, by cords provided for the purpose, she was prevented from rising. I besought--I threatened--I raved;--but all thoughts and minds were engrossed by the premature fate of one so young and beautiful, and I was unheeded.

"Among the relatives who pressed around the funeral pile, I saw Balty Mahu; and indignation for a moment got the better of grief. The pile was now lighted, and in a moment all was hidden in smoke. I sickened at the sight, and was obliged to turn away. Even then I heard, or thought I heard, the dying shrieks of the victim, amid the groans and cries, and the thousand shouts that rent the air! The pile and its contents being now enveloped in flame, my keepers set me free, when, by an impulse of frenzy, I rushed' to the pile, to make a last vain effort to rescue Veenah, or to share her fate; but was stopped by some of the bystanders, who called my act a profanation.

"'Yes,' said Balty Mahu, 'he has always been a scoffer of our religion.' As soon as these words reached my ears, with the quickness of thought I snatched a cimeter from the hands of one of the guards, and plunged it in his breast. Of all that happened afterwards, my recollection is very confused. I was rudely seized, and hurried to prison. My father was coming to meet me, when he was informed of the fatal deed. I remember that my coolness, or rather stupor, was in strong contrast with the violence of his emotion. He accompanied me to prison, and continued with me that night.

"It is not easy to take the life of one of my caste in India; and, by dint of the exertions of my friends, in spite of the influence of Shunah Shoo, and the family of the Omrah, I was pardoned, on condition of doing penance, which was, that I should never live in a country in which the religion of Brahmin prevailed, and should not again look at, or converse with, any woman for two minutes together. Ere this took place, my excellent mother, unable to withstand the shocks she had received from my supposed death, my misfortunes, and my crime, died a martyr to maternal affection. Wishing to conform to the sentence, and to be as near my father as I could, I removed to the kingdom of Ava, where, you know, they are followers of Buddha. Here I continued as long as my father lived, which was about six years. In this period, time had so alleviated my grief, that I began to take pleasure in the cultivation of science, which constituted my chief employment.

"After my father's death, I indulged a curiosity I had felt in my youth, of seeing foreign countries; and I visited China, Japan, and England. During my residence in Asia, I had discovered lunarium ore in the mountain near Mogaun; and this circumstance, many years afterwards, when I determined to rest from my labours, induced me to settle in that mountain, as I have before stated. I have occasionally used the metal to counterbalance the gravity of a small car, by which I have profited, by a favourable wind, to indulge the melancholy satisfaction of looking down on the tombs of my parents, and of the ill-fated Veenah: approaching the earth near enough, in the night, to see the sacred spots, but not enough to violate the religious injunctions of my caste; to avoid which, however, it was sometimes necessary for me to go across Hindostan to Arabia or Persia, and there wait for a change of wind before I could return: and it was these excursions which suggested to the superstitious Burmans that my form had undergone a temporary transformation. When such have been the woes of my life, you can no longer think it strange, Atterley, that I delayed their painful recital; or that, after having endured so much, all common dangers and misfortunes should appear to me insignificant."

*   *   *   *   *

The venerable Brahmin here concluded his narrative, and we both remained thoughtful and silent for some time; he, apparently absorbed in the recollections of his eventful life; and I, partly in the reflections awakened by his story, and partly in the intense interest of revisiting my native earth, and beholding once more all who were dear to me. Already the extended map beneath us was assuming a distinct and varied appearance; and the Brahmin, having applied his eye to the telescope, and made a brief calculation of our progress, considered that twenty-four hours more, if no accident interrupted us, would end our voyage; part of which interval I passed in making notes in my journal, and in contemplating the different sections of our many-peopled globe, as they presented themselves successively to the eye. It was my wish to land on the American continent, and, if possible, in the United States. But the Brahmin put an end to that hope, by reminding me that we should be attracted towards the Equator, and that we had to choose between Asia, Africa, and South America; and that our only course would be, to check the progress of our car over the country of greatest extent, through which the equinoctial circle might pass. Saying which, he relapsed into his melancholy silence, and I betook myself once more to the telescope. With a bosom throbbing with emotion, I saw that we were descending towards the American continent. When we were about ten or twelve miles from the earth, the Brahmin arrested the progress of the car, and we hovered over the broad Atlantic. Looking down on the ocean, the first object which presented itself to my eye, was a small one-masted shallop, which was buffeting the waves in a south-westerly direction. I presumed it was a New England trader, on a voyage to some part of the Republic of Colombia: and, by way of diverting my friend from his melancholy reverie, I told him some of the many stories which are current respecting the enterprise and ingenuity of this portion of my countrymen, and above all, their adroitness at a bargain.

"Methinks," says the Brahmin, "you are describing a native of Canton or Pekin. But," added he, after a short pause, "though to a superficial observer man appears to put on very different characters, to a philosopher he is every where the same--for he is every where moulded by the circumstances in which he is placed. Thus; let him be in a situation that is propitious to commerce, and the habits of traffic produce in him shrewdness and address. Trade is carried on chiefly in towns, because it is there carried on most advantageously. This situation gives the trader a more intimate knowledge of his species--a more ready insight into character, and of the modes of operating on it. His chief purpose is to buy as cheap, and to sell as dear, as he can; and he is often able to heighten the recommendations or soften the defects of some of the articles in which he deals, without danger of immediate detection; or, in other words, his representations have some influence with his customers. He avails himself of this circumstance, and thus acquires the habit of lying; but, as he is studious to conceal it, he becomes wary, ingenious, and cunning. It is thus that the Phenicians, the Carthagenians, the Dutch, the Chinese, the New-Englanders, and the modern Greeks, have always been regarded as inclined to petty frauds by their less commercial neighbours." I mentioned the English nation.

"If the English," said he, interrupting me, "who are the most commercial people of modern times, have not acquired the same character, it is because they are as distinguished for other things as for traffic: they are not merely a commercial people--they are also agricultural, warlike, and literary; and thus the natural tendencies of commerce are mutually counteracted."

We afterwards descended slowly; the prospect beneath us becoming more beautiful than my humble pen can hope to describe, or will even attempt to portray. In a short time after, we were in sight of Venezuela. We met with the trade-winds, and were carried by them forty or fifty miles inland, where, with some difficulty, and even danger, we landed. The Brahmin and myself remained together two days, and parted--he to explore the Andes, to obtain additional light on the subject of his hypothesis, and I, on the wings of impatience, to visit once more my long-deserted family and friends. But before our separation, I assisted my friend in concealing our aerial vessel, and received a promise from him to visit, and perhaps spend with me the evening of his life. Of my journey home, little remains to be said. From the citizens of Colombia, I experienced kindness and attention, and means of conveyance to Caraccas; where, embarking on board the brig Juno, captain Withers, I once more set foot in New York, on the 18th of August, 1826, after an absence of four years, resolved, for the rest of my life, to travel only in books, and persuaded, from experience, that the satisfaction which the wanderer gains from actually beholding the wonders and curiosities of distant climes, is dearly bought by the sacrifice of all the comforts and delights of home.

The Codes Of Hammurabi And Moses
W. W. Davies

QTY

The discovery of the Hammurabi Code is one of the greatest achievements of archaeology, and is of paramount interest, not only to the student of the Bible, but also to all those interested in ancient history...

Religion   **ISBN:** *1-59462-338-4*   **Pages:132**

MSRP $12.95

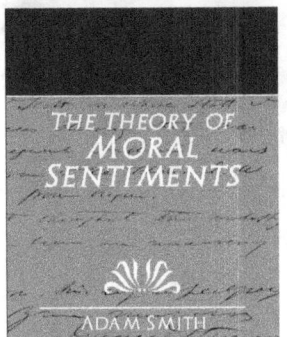

The Theory of Moral Sentiments
Adam Smith

QTY

This work from 1749. contains original theories of conscience amd moral judgment and it is the foundation for systemof morals.

Philosophy   **ISBN:** *1-59462-777-0*   **Pages:536**

MSRP $19.95

Jessica's First Prayer
Hesba Stretton

QTY

In a screened and secluded corner of one of the many railway-bridges which span the streets of London there could be seen a few years ago, from five o'clock every morning until half past eight, a tidily set-out coffee-stall, consisting of a trestle and board, upon which stood two large tin cans, with a small fire of charcoal burning under each so as to keep the coffee boiling during the early hours of the morning when the work-people were thronging into the city on their way to their daily toil...

Childrens   **ISBN:** *1-59462-373-2*   **Pages:84**

MSRP $9.95

My Life and Work
Henry Ford

QTY

Henry Ford revolutionized the world with his implementation of mass production for the Model T automobile. Gain valuable business insight into his life and work with his own auto-biography... "We have only started on our development of our country we have not as yet, with all our talk of wonderful progress, done more than scratch the surface. The progress has been wonderful enough but..."

Biographies/   **ISBN:** *1-59462-198-5*   **Pages:300**

MSRP $21.95

The Art of Cross-Examination
Francis Wellman

QTY

I presume it is the experience of every author, after his first book is published upon an important subject, to be almost overwhelmed with a wealth of ideas and illustrations which could readily have been included in his book, and which to his own mind, at least, seem to make a second edition inevitable. Such certainly was the case with me; and when the first edition had reached its sixth impression in five months, I rejoiced to learn that it seemed to my publishers that the book had met with a sufficiently favorable reception to justify a second and considerably enlarged edition. ..

Reference   ISBN: *1-59462-647-2*

Pages:412

MSRP $19.95

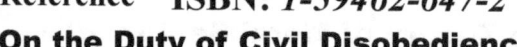

On the Duty of Civil Disobedience
Henry David Thoreau

QTY

Thoreau wrote his famous essay, On the Duty of Civil Disobedience, as a protest against an unjust but popular war and the immoral but popular institution of slave-owning. He did more than write—he declined to pay his taxes, and was hauled off to gaol in consequence. Who can say how much this refusal of his hastened the end of the war and of slavery ?

Law   ISBN: *1-59462-747-9*

Pages:48

MSRP $7.45

Dream Psychology Psychoanalysis for Beginners
Sigmund Freud

QTY

Sigmund Freud, born Sigismund Schlomo Freud (May 6, 1856 - September 23, 1939), was a Jewish-Austrian neurologist and psychiatrist who co-founded the psychoanalytic school of psychology. Freud is best known for his theories of the unconscious mind, especially involving the mechanism of repression; his redefinition of sexual desire as mobile and directed towards a wide variety of objects; and his therapeutic techniques, especially his understanding of transference in the therapeutic relationship and the presumed value of dreams as sources of insight into unconscious desires.

Psychology   ISBN: *1-59462-905-6*

Pages:196

MSRP $15.45

The Miracle of Right Thought
Orison Swett Marden

QTY

Believe with all of your heart that you will do what you were made to do. When the mind has once formed the habit of holding cheerful, happy, prosperous pictures, it will not be easy to form the opposite habit. It does not matter how improbable or how far away this realization may see, or how dark the prospects may be, if we visualize them as best we can, as vividly as possible, hold tenaciously to them and vigorously struggle to attain them, they will gradually become actualized, realized in the life. But a desire, a longing without endeavor, a yearning abandoned or held indifferently will vanish without realization.

Self Help   ISBN: *1-59462-644-8*

Pages:360

MSRP $25.45

QTY

The Rosicrucian Cosmo-Conception Mystic Christianity by *Max Heindel*   ISBN: *1-59462-188-8* **$38.95**
The Rosicrucian Cosmo-conception is not dogmatic, neither does it appeal to any other authority than the reason of the student. It is: not controversial,
but is: sent forth in the, hope that it may help to clear..   New Age/Religion Pages 646

Abandonment To Divine Providence by *Jean-Pierre de Caussade*   ISBN: *1-59462-228-0* **$25.95**
"The Rev. Jean Pierre de Caussade was one of the most remarkable spiritual writers of the Society of Jesus in France in the 18th Century. His death took
place at Toulouse in 1751. His works have gone through many editions and have been republished...   Inspirational/Religion Pages 400

Mental Chemistry by *Charles Haanel*   ISBN: *1-59462-192-6* **$23.95**
Mental Chemistry allows the change of material conditions by combining and appropriately utilizing the power of the mind. Much like applied chemistry
creates something new and unique out of careful combinations of chemicals the mastery of mental chemistry...   New Age/Business Pages 354

The Letters of Robert Browning and Elizabeth Barret Barrett 1845-1846 vol II   ISBN: *1-59462-193-4* **$35.95**
by *Robert Browning* and *Elizabeth Barrett*   Biographies Pages 596

Gleanings In Genesis (volume I) by *Arthur W. Pink*   ISBN: *1-59462-130-6* **$27.45**
Appropriately has Genesis been termed "the seed plot of the Bible" for in it we have, in germ form, almost all of the great doctrines which are afterwards
fully developed in the books of Scripture which follow...   Religion/Inspirational Pages 420

The Master Key by *L. W. de Laurence*   ISBN: *1-59462-001-6* **$30.95**
In no branch of human knowledge has there been a more lively increase of the spirit of research during the past few years than in the study of Psychology,
Concentration and Mental Discipline. The requests for authentic lessons in Thought Control, Mental Discipline and...   New Age/Business Pages 422

The Lesser Key Of Solomon Goetia by *L. W. de Laurence*   ISBN: *1-59462-092-X* **$9.95**
This translation of the first book of the "Lernegton" which is now for the first time made accessible to students of Talismanic Magic was done, after careful
collation and edition, from numerous Ancient Manuscripts in Hebrew, Latin, and French...   New Age/Occult Pages 92

Rubaiyat Of Omar Khayyam by *Edward Fitzgerald*   ISBN:*1-59462-332-5* **$13.95**
Edward Fitzgerald, whom the world has already learned, in spite of his own efforts to remain within the shadow of anonymity, to look upon as one of the
rarest poets of the century, was born at Bredfield, in Suffolk, on the 31st of March, 1809. He was the third son of John Purcell...   Music Pages 172

Ancient Law by *Henry Maine*   ISBN: *1-59462-128-4* **$29.95**
The chief object of the following pages is to indicate some of the earliest ideas of mankind, as they are reflected in Ancient Law, and to point out the
relation of those ideas to modern thought.   Religiom/History Pages 452

Far-Away Stories by *William J. Locke*   ISBN: *1-59462-129-2* **$19.45**
"Good wine needs no bush, but a collection of mixed vintages does. And this book is just such a collection. Some of the stories I do not want to remain
buried for ever in the museum files of dead magazine-numbers an author's not unpardonable vanity..."   Fiction Pages 272

Life of David Crockett by *David Crockett*   ISBN: *1-59462-250-7* **$27.45**
"Colonel David Crockett was one of the most remarkable men of the times in which he lived. Born in humble life, but gifted with a strong will, an
indomitable courage, and unremitting perseverance...   Biographies/New Age Pages 424

Lip-Reading by *Edward Nitchie*   ISBN: *1-59462-206-X* **$25.95**
Edward B. Nitchie, founder of the New York School for the Hard of Hearing, now the Nitchie School of Lip-Reading, Inc, wrote "LIP-READING Principles
and Practice". The development and perfecting of this meritorious work on lip-reading was an undertaking...   How-to Pages 400

A Handbook of Suggestive Therapeutics, Applied Hypnotism, Psychic Science   ISBN: *1-59462-214-0* **$24.95**
by *Henry Munro*   Health/New Age/Health/Self-help Pages 376

A Doll's House: and Two Other Plays by *Henrik Ibsen*   ISBN: *1-59462-112-8* **$19.95**
Henrik Ibsen created this classic when in revolutionary 1848 Rome. Introducing some striking concepts in playwriting for the realist genre, this play
has been studied the world over.   Fiction/Classics/Plays 308

The Light of Asia by *sir Edwin Arnold*   ISBN: *1-59462-204-3* **$13.95**
In this poetic masterpiece, Edwin Arnold describes the life and teachings of Buddha. The man who was to become known as Buddha to the world was
born as Prince Gautama of India but he rejected the worldly riches and abandoned the reigns of power when... Religion/History/Biographies Pages 170

The Complete Works of Guy de Maupassant by *Guy de Maupassant*   ISBN: *1-59462-157-8* **$16.95**
"For days and days, nights and nights, I had dreamed of that first kiss which was to consecrate our engagement, and I knew not on what spot I should
put my lips..."   Fiction/Classics Pages 240

The Art of Cross-Examination by *Francis L. Wellman*   ISBN: *1-59462-309-0* **$26.95**
Written by a renowned trial lawyer, Wellman imparts his experience and uses case studies to explain how to use psychology to extract desired information
through questioning.   How-to/Science/Reference Pages 408

Answered or Unanswered? by *Louisa Vaughan*   ISBN: *1-59462-248-5* **$10.95**
Miracles of Faith in China   Religion Pages 112

The Edinburgh Lectures on Mental Science (1909) by *Thomas*   ISBN: *1-59462-008-3* **$11.95**
This book contains the substance of a course of lectures recently given by the writer in the Queen Street Hail, Edinburgh. Its purpose is to indicate the
Natural Principles governing the relation between Mental Action and Material Conditions...   New Age/Psychology Pages 148

Ayesha by *H. Rider Haggard*   ISBN: *1-59462-301-5* **$24.95**
Verily and indeed it is the unexpected that happens! Probably if there was one person upon the earth from whom the Editor of this, and of a certain previ-
ous history, did not expect to hear again...   Classics Pages 380

Ayala's Angel by *Anthony Trollope*   ISBN: *1-59462-352-X* **$29.95**
The two girls were both pretty, but Lucy who was twenty-one who supposed to be simple and comparatively unattractive, whereas Ayala was credited, as
her Bombwhat romantic name might show, with poetic charm and a taste for romance. Ayala when her father died was nineteen...   Fiction Pages 484

The American Commonwealth by *James Bryce*   ISBN: *1-59462-286-8* **$34.45**
An interpretation of American democratic political theory. It examines political mechanics and society from the perspective of Scotsman
James Bryce   Politics Pages 572

Stories of the Pilgrims by *Margaret P. Pumphrey*   ISBN: *1-59462-116-0* **$17.95**
This book explores pilgrims religious oppression in England as well as their escape to Holland and eventual crossing to America on the Mayflower, and
their early days in New England...   History Pages 268

QTY

The Fasting Cure *by Sinclair Upton*   ISBN: *1-59462-222-1*   **$13.95**
In the Cosmopolitan Magazine for May, 1910, and in the Contemporary Review (London) for April, 1910, I published an article dealing with my experiences in fasting. I have written a great many magazine articles, but never one which attracted so much attention...   New Age/Self Help/Health Pages 164

Hebrew Astrology *by Sepharial*   ISBN: *1-59462-308-2*   **$13.45**
In these days of advanced thinking it is a matter of common observation that we have left many of the old landmarks behind and that we are now pressing forward to greater heights and to a wider horizon than that which represented the mind-content of our progenitors...   Astrology Pages 144

Thought Vibration or The Law of Attraction in the Thought World   ISBN: *1-59462-127-6*   **$12.95**
by William Walker Atkinson   *Psychology/Religion Pages 144*

Optimism *by Helen Keller*   ISBN: *1-59462-108-X*   **$15.95**
Helen Keller was blind, deaf, and mute since 19 months old, yet famously learned how to overcome these handicaps, communicate with the world, and spread her lectures promoting optimism. An inspiring read for everyone...   Biographies/Inspirational Pages 84

Sara Crewe *by Frances Burnett*   ISBN: *1-59462-360-0*   **$9.45**
In the first place, Miss Minchin lived in London. Her home was a large, dull, tall one, in a large, dull square, where all the houses were alike, and all the sparrows were alike, and where all the door-knockers made the same heavy sound...   Childrens/Classic Pages 88

The Autobiography of Benjamin Franklin *by Benjamin Franklin*   ISBN: *1-59462-135-7*   **$24.95**
The Autobiography of Benjamin Franklin has probably been more extensively read than any other American historical work, and no other book of its kind has had such ups and downs of fortune. Franklin lived for many years in England, where he was agent...   Biographies/History Pages 332

Name	
Email	
Telephone	
Address	
City, State ZIP	

☐ **Credit Card**   ☐ **Check / Money Order**

Credit Card Number	
Expiration Date	
Signature	

Please Mail to: Book Jungle
PO Box 2226
Champaign, IL 61825
or Fax to: 630-214-0564

ORDERING INFORMATION

web: *www.bookjungle.com*
email: *sales@bookjungle.com*
fax: *630-214-0564*
mail: *Book Jungle PO Box 2226 Champaign, IL 61825*
or PayPal *to sales@bookjungle.com*

Please contact us for bulk discounts

DIRECT-ORDER TERMS

**20% Discount if You Order
Two or More Books**
Free Domestic Shipping!
Accepted: Master Card, Visa,
Discover, American Express

www.ingramcontent.com/pod-product-compliance
Lightning Source LLC
Chambersburg PA
CBHW080735250626
47170CB00010B/2836